The

Perfect

Fig

By

S. M. Walker

These are works of fiction. Names, characters, places and incidents either are the product of my imagination or are used fictitiously, and any resemblance to actual persons, living or dead, businesses, companies, events or locales, is entirely coincidental.

The comments beneath the stories are all true, to the best of my knowledge.

For Dad, Fred Walker, a good and happy man who loved others as himself. I miss his kindness and his wise words.

And, for Matteo Federico Saveri, my son, my Sun. With gratitude, love and admiration.

"How many of us live lives of quiet desperation… we hope to be saved by one person, one thing, we convince ourselves that one thing can last."

Alexander McCall Smith, *The Unbearable Lightness of Scones*

Contents

Preface

I'm still here in Tursi, living in a little stone house in a medieval hamlet on a hill in Basilicata, in Italy's Deep South. Coming here was a bit of a culture shock after living for many years in the North of Italy. The journey, in a van full of oranges on April Fool's Day was, erm, eventful!

When I'm not writing, I'm with my totally crazy and wonderful friend Martine, having adventures and getting ideas for more stories. The weather is cooler. The doors to the balcony are always open and there is a lovely breeze whispering across the valley. It's September, my favourite month.

Mornings are the best time for sitting outside with my black Labrador, Harley, drinking coffee and reading through my notebooks. The view across to the 15th Century Convent of San

Francesco D'Assisi never ceases to fascinate me. Every day there is a different sunrise in a different sky and each one is truly beautiful. My neighbours continue to give me fruit every time I go out. They all stop to chat. Life is slow. Life is good.

This book, like the previous one, *The Wife in the Wardrobe*, is a collection of short and very short stories put together from thoughts and stories written in my many notebooks over a period of about five years, and a few new ones. I decided to add, this time, a few words about how the ideas for the story came to me.

Stories do have a tendency to write themselves though, and I find it best to let them go where they wish to go. I hope you enjoy reading them as much as I have enjoyed writing them.

The title, *The Perfect Fig*, came to Martine when I told her what had happened to me one day. I reached up to pick a fig from the low hanging branches of the tree that grows on my terrace. The sun was going down and in the dusky light, I realised as I touched it that it was not a fig at all but one of the lightbulbs on the strings threaded through the canopy of branches. I hope nobody saw me laughing hysterically to myself.

Toad in the Hole

'Cheaters never change their spots!' Rosemary tried to console her best friend, Davina. They were having afternoon tea at the new garden centre that had opened just outside the village on the old road to Lower Fromsley. Despite her feelings of desperation at Donald's appalling behaviour, Davina somehow managed to pop a tiny square of millionaire's shortbread into her mouth. She then began to eye up the scones. It had been hours since lunch and she was feeling rather peckish.

Davina and Donald had not been married long. They'd had a lovely ceremony at Donald's family estate in Dunbartonshire and had honeymooned in Paris. It was something of a cliché, but Donald was Davina's third husband and she was his fourth (and final, so he declared), bride.

It was rather difficult to find somewhere that neither of them had visited on honeymoon!

Then again, perhaps it wasn't that important to go somewhere different. Davina's sister, Kate, had married her second husband at the same church as the first – St. Swithun's on the Fold – and on the same date. They had held the reception at the same venue and gone on honeymoon to the same hotel on the same Greek island. Davina had asked whether Graham hadn't been disturbed by this. Apparently, he had not.

Kate said it made it so much easier to remember everything. Davina was not convinced. She thought, in fact, that it would have made things very confusing. She declared that she would never have been able to remember what had happened when and with whom. Kate shrugged and said, 'well, it's done now. No going back. When I marry again, I plan on doing the same'. Davina had been alarmed. Poor Graham. Was his successor already in the pipeline? One could never know with Kate. Graham really was a spiffing brother-in-law. Much better than *Wotsisname*, the first one. She pondered on how easy it was to forget someone once they had been replaced.

Now, only five months after she had wandered around the little side streets of Paris, hand-in-hand with Donald and gazed in awe at the Mona Lisa, albeit behind glass, she had caught him cheating on her. And, to add insult to injury, he had had the audacity to admit it. He could have at least tried to deny it, allowing her the opportunity of pretending that it wasn't happening, had that been her wont. Davina was not sure if it was. Donald had even used that old excuse that, having made his mistress his wife, there was a vacancy. Apparently, the vacancy for a new mistress had been filled by Abigail, the butcher's daughter. A meaty, young and mousey-haired girl with an enormous bosom. She was the sausage filler.

Davina was trying very hard to be indignant but, on the whole, she realised that she was experiencing something akin to relief. She was not keen on Donald's cack-handed fumblings in the dark. She was, if truth be told, coming round to the idea of handing his *needs* over to Abigail. She wondered, though, if there were a way of using the situation to her advantage, (she was, after all, a thrifty Scottish lady).

As she bit into a frangipane slice, she decided that, once afternoon tea was over (it would be jolly rude of her to leave dear old Rosemary alone with all these cakes), she would march round to the butcher's shop and demand a discount on Abigail's best bangers.

She rather fancied some links of Lincolnshire with herby sage and perhaps a coil or two of Cumberland. She would tell cook to prepare a lovely toad-in-the-hole for supper. Bliss. She hadn't enjoyed a good banger in a long while. It was the perfect solution. They could both have their sausage and eat it!

Rosemary poured more tea and smiled. Her friend was looking cheerier already.

***

The idea for this story came about because I was missing certain things about the UK when I moved to Italy. I miss garden centres and afternoon tea and cooked breakfasts. Though, when I lived in the UK, I never ate a cooked breakfast! I worked long hours at the university. I liked my job. I liked the university. I went in early and stayed late. I was in a netball team. We were terrible. I went swimming in my lunch break. I ate sandwiches from the little shop in the main square, queueing for ages. I always wondered why they never opened another shop, or made that one bigger. I appreciate efficiency and the maximization of potential.

I had a distinct lack of time and used to eat toast for breakfast (like most people), with lashings of butter. We always had butter in our house. I never ate margarine. That is probably because my father had once been a dairy farmer. It was long before I was born but most of his friends were farming folk. I spent a lot of time on farms and in farmhouse kitchens. Farmhouse kitchens with warm AGAs and chairs with curled up cats, and dogs lying on rugs are my idea of home and love and happiness.

In any case, despite never eating sausage, bacon and eggs and such like in the UK, when I moved to Italy, I began to miss a nice cooked breakfast. I realised that it is possible to miss something that you have rarely had. I cannot say never, as we used to stop at the motorway services and have a cooked breakfast when we went on holiday as a child. It was a special treat.

After moving to Italy, I returned home often and always stayed with various family members. I have a very large family. Then, after getting married to an Italian, I returned often to see my English family but took advantage of the chance to travel around the UK staying in various Bed and Breakfast establishments. And so, my love of cooked breakfasts exploded. I crave them often. Italian sausages are not breakfast fayre. The bacon is not the same, though after many *baconless* years, there is now something similar. Eggs are eggs I guess. Though some would disagree. In life there are always some who disagree. It is a good thing. It would not do for us to be all alike.

I cannot actually remember having ever eaten toad in the hole. I do love a good Yorkshire pudding though. Especially with roast beef. Am I a traitor to my native Lancashire because of this? I do not think so. Everybody loves Yorkshire puddings, don't they?

Another thing I miss about the UK is Christmas.

Crackers

'We need to decide on the bird.'

'What bird would that be darling?'

'The bird for Christmas. We need to decide whether to get a guinea fowl or a goose.'

'But, it's August!'

'I know. We need to get a move on and decide.'

We're sitting on the beach near our home in the South of Italy. It's forty-two degrees and my wife is thinking about Christmas. My wife is English. She loves to be organised. Even so…

I apply more sun cream, lie back in my sun-lounger and close my eyes. I contemplate putting my flip-flops on and going for a quick swim to cool down but my wife is now asking me about Christmas Pudding. I say what I always say when she talks to me about pudding. It is the reason why there are so many widows in England. The women there use spotted dick and treacle pudding and jam roly-poly to kill their husbands. I've always said that the way to a man's heart attack is through his pudding.

Henrietta has decided that we will be spending this Christmas in Italy. We usually go to England to be with her, rather large, family in Dorset. The sun is burning my shins as I apply more factor 30 and reflect on Christmases past.

Our first Christmas in England was before we were married. We stayed with Etta's parents in their gorgeous cottage near Dorchester. It was my first visit to England. I'd been to Scotland, to Edinburgh to be precise, with my ex-girlfriend, Cinzia, but Etta had not been pleased to hear how much fun we'd had when I mentioned it once. (I had not expected so much jealousy from an English girl. I thought she would have been more cold-blooded.)

Edinburgh in summer was a jolt to all the senses. It was hot and cold, and dry and damp. It was loud and impressive, and crazy. It was joy. There was some kind of weird festival. We could not understand the locals nor the performers but we were caught up and carried along by the laughter and the fun.

We stayed in a B&B with a proprietor who loved to talk about the weather. He was incredibly tall, with long and oddly straight legs, which didn't seem to bend when he walked, resulting in a somewhat military march through the breakfast room. Each morning he would ask us how we'd slept and tell us the weather forecast for the day. Then he would arrive with huge hot plates of bacon, square sausages, egg and fried bread. There were baked beans. I tried them but asked to be spared them in future. Italians do not eat beans at

20

breakfast. Then again, nor do they eat sausage and bacon!

Cinzia ate everything. We were eighteen and she had the appetite of a horse. A very slim horse who never gained weight. By mid morning, she would be hungry again and I was required to accompany her to many a Scottish bakery. While I sipped my foul watery coffee, each day she would munch her way happily through an assortment of delicacies such as fudge-topped salted caramel muffins, white chocolate brownies with ice cream and various pastries, doughnuts and buns. By the end of our twelve-day stay, I think she had tried every cake known to Scotland and approved whole-heartedly of them all.

As we couldn't understand a great deal of the comedy, we were drawn to the more visual exhibitions and performances going on in the centre, such as dance and circus and theatre. The crowds and the noise and the colour filled us with excitement. Great blazes of red and yellow and orange. Great blasts of music and song. People pushing and shoving politely with lots of *sorrys* and gentle coughs. Then, tired and happy, we would set off on the rather long walk back to our bizarre B&B with the purple door and the brass thistle door knocker. Back to our small soft bed with crisp white sheets and our plug-in kettle and sachets of Nescafé and tiny basket of herbal teas.

Everything was fun and everything was funny. We were young and thought we were in love. We laughed at everything. We laughed at men in kilts playing (very loud) bagpipes. We laughed at clowns and jugglers. We ate fish and *chups* and drank Irn-Bru as we looked out across the harbour at the lighthouse and the dark sea and laughed at the biting wind whipping our hair across our faces. We enjoyed the anonymity and the freedom of being tourists.

'Of course, I'll have to order crackers. I don't know if you can still get them online. Explosives and all that...' My wife was still planning Christmas. I remembered the hilarity of my first encounter with Christmas crackers, the unfunny jokes, the useless plastic toys, the paper hats. I rather liked wearing a paper crown to eat my lunch and threw myself into this weird custom with enthusiasm. My soon-to-be father-in-law had kept his hat on all day. Through the Queen's speech and even when he fell asleep in his armchair.

'I must get my sister to post some of those chocolate mints Aunt Dotty always has.' My wife is happy planning. Perhaps I should just leave her to it and be grateful. We have a wonderful life, great meals and lovely holidays and a nice home and garden mostly because my wife is a planner. I am well aware that there are worse things in life than an organised wife.

I put my designer flip-flops on and walk through the rows of beach-lovers under umbrellas to take a quick dip in the sea. All this talk of Christmas food has made me hungry. I think about having a leisurely lunch in the restaurant overlooking the beach with my wife. I should do so much more to make her happy.

When I come out of the sea, I am completely disorientated. Each umbrella is the same as its neighbour. I'm not sure if my wife and my clothes are to the right or to the left of me. I suppose we must have been assigned a number when we paid this morning. I try to remember it, but my wife had taken care of that, as usual. I try and establish my position by finding something familiar. All the little pathways back from the sea look the same.

My embarrassment, at not knowing where our umbrella is, is starting to escalate into panic. I find my flip-flops and try to think back to the path I had taken, heading vaguely in the direction of the bar. I think we were in row five or six. Without my glasses on, I cannot read the numbers on the umbrella poles in any case.

Just as I decide to go to the bar and phone my wife to tell her I am lost, I see her standing by our sun-loungers waving at me with both arms. She looks like one of those guys who stand on the runway directing planes. All she needs is a bright orange plastic waistcoat. I saunter back to her nonchalantly. I know she knows I was lost but I pretend that I wasn't anyway. She laughs as I dry myself off on my towel and lie down next to her. She looks happy. My wife is almost always happy.

She tells me that she's just had a phone call from her sister. Astrid is getting married on 20th December, a bit last minute but there was a cancellation at the venue and the vicar had apparently managed to fit them in too.

'We could stay over for Christmas,' I suggest. My wife smiles and says she had hoped that I would say that. She puts her list back in her bag and lies down on her sun-lounger. I reach out and hold her hand. I love her so much. I'm glad she won't have to plan Christmas now.

'I wonder what colour scheme Astrid has chosen,' my wife says. 'I'll have to buy my dress here in Italy. I think the little ones will be bridesmaids.' My wife takes out her notepad again and starts to write down things to do before we go to the wedding. I don't mind. I smile to myself. I really would be lost without her.

***

My mother adored Christmas. (Not the mother who disliked me, another mother. It is a long and complicated story but I am trying to tell it.) We always had lots of presents and lots of food and lots of people. My family is rather large.

When I was a girl, I lived in a beautiful Georgian house on a private terrace above the main road going into town. I thought that we were rich. It turned out that we were not. It had four floors. I think the cellar had a white door but that may have been one of the other houses I have lived in. I know that there was a coal chute into it as one of my cousins fell down it when she was little. Poor thing. I think she broke her nose, though I may have imagined that as well. We do have a tendency to rewrite memories, don't we? Well, *I* do. I have always had a bad memory and the things I remember are often confused along with other things. Some of them happened and some of them didn't. In my mind, they did and that is all that is important to me. I never have been pedantic.

We had a small garden at the front of the house. The neighbours had an antique birdbath. We had a lawn. My father once paved a kind of maize around the other side of the garden from the lawn and planted roses. He loved roses. I have never liked flowers. I like things that are green. Trees and bushes and grass and cacti but I am not keen on flowers. I cannot remember ever having had a bad experience with them. I just dislike them. Especially roses. I suppose, if I had to have flowers, I would choose dog daisies.

There were two living areas to the front of the house, both with long windows. It was a rather symmetrical house, like the ones children draw. A door in the middle and a window each side and above, three windows and a roof with a chimney. In my drawings, there was a sun in the corner and smoke coming out of the chimney. We had fireplaces but I don't think we ever used them, so there would not have been smoke. There probably would not have been sun either. Though, in my childhood memories, it was always sunny.

Various family members and their husbands/wives/girlfriends/cats etc. used one of the two front rooms, and my parents and I used the other. Though it was always full of visitors in any case. Over the years, the décor changed. I remember it when it had a purple shagpile carpet, orange crushed velvet curtains, and an enormous cream sofa and chairs. It was the seventies! The ceilings had original crown moldings and plaster work. I didn't realise just how beautiful they were.

The dining room, to the back of the house, looked out onto a rather sad little yard. I used to play there sometimes, though I preferred the orchard beyond it. I have happy memories of rotten apple fights. I once popped my head around the high gate, thought I was safe and got hit in the stomach by an apple which exploded all over my new Sunday dress. I was too afraid to tell my mother so I hung it in the wardrobe and promptly forgot about it. The following Sunday all hell let loose. My mother bought me another dress with Greenshield stamps. It was my job to lick the back of them and stick them into books. I must have swallowed an awful lot of glue over the years.

I cannot remember the Christmases there very well. We left when I was eleven. The house was too big after everyone had got married and moved out. We moved into a small house with only three bedrooms. It felt like a bit of a comedown. My grandmother moved in with us. They said she had dementia.

One Christmas, I remember sneaking downstairs very early to open my presents and wrap them back up before anyone got up. I only had a few bits. A poor show. When I opened them again, I pretended to be surprised. My real surprise was a lovely red bike behind the door. I loved that bike and cycled everywhere. Up and down the cobbled streets and into town. I once cycled with my younger sisters and cousins all the way to

Morecambe. We were exhausted and got back late for dinner. My mother was furious. There were no mobile phones then and people didn't check where their children were. I got the blame, of course. I also got cold and salty beef stew with lumps of carrot.

In the Dark

The fact that he couldn't see me with his eyes made me feel nervous. I always had the sensation that he could *see* something more. Something deeper and more intimate. The way he touched me made me feel too naked. It made me feel vulnerable. The way he touched me excited me so much. I imagined that he was imagining me, and that made me scared and turned on at the same time.

Grant and I had met through mutual friends. Adina and Roger had known we would hit it off. Adina was my florist and Roger, well, Roger was just Roger. A kind and gentle man with a love of tropical fish. He was widely read and could, and did, wax lyrical on any subject for hours. He liked to wear bow ties, often red. His favourite one was dark red silk with tiny blue and white spots. He had been wearing it on the evening on which I had been invited to dinner. (I soon realised that I was the object of a little light matchmaking, as was Grant.)

After losing his sight, over time, Grant's other senses had become heightened. He spoke quite freely and openly about his accident and the way his life had changed. I found his courage inspirational and thought that, when my time came to face tragedy, I would not be so brave.

He loved music and had eclectic tastes. He loved both Irish folk songs and Opera (his favourite was Turandot). He often sang *Nessun dorma* in the shower, *Vincerò, Vincerò*! And I knew that he *would* win, he *would* overcome all adversity because that was the man he was. The man I was falling in love with.

I was falling in love with him quickly, easily, naturally. It was gentle and it was passionate. I felt like I was floating on a cloud. I hadn't ever dreamt that a love like ours could exist. I really had thought that it was only for books and films. When we were together, I was happy. I adapted my days and my plans for the future to fit in with him and his desires.

Of course, it wasn't simple having a partner who was blind. He was independent and strong but there were things he couldn't do and there were people who judged us. I became accustomed to being observed discretely, and sometimes not very discretely, in restaurants and shopping centres. I was glad that when we were out and about, Grant could not see the looks of pity on the faces passing by. I accepted that there were things that were difficult to do together. It was not a sacrifice. I felt blessed to be able to accommodate him into my life.

I am an artist. I spend my days with my hair tied up on top of my head and my sleeves rolled up. My world is a world of colour. I cannot imagine how I would feel to lose orange, to lose pink, to lose yellow. I am afraid when I try to consider what it must be like to lead a life where everything is black. I am unable and unwilling to do it. Colour makes me happy. It affects my mood. In black I feel sad. In yellow I feel full of life and energy. I wish I could bring myself to talk more to Grant about this, but it is difficult. I don't want to be indelicate.

Grant lost his sight only a few years ago in an explosion. One of those freak accidents. He still remembers colour. I wonder if that is a blessing or a curse. I describe my orange, turquoise and fuchsia-pink works to him in detail. I describe the great canvases of coloured vases and coloured flowers and coloured backgrounds. He loves the fact that *my* world is full of colour. He is pensive but supportive.

He came with me to the opening evening of my latest exhibition. The previous day, we had gone to the venue and I had walked him round the layout and explained to him where all the paintings were. He had listened carefully to my description of the composition and colour. He had seemed happy enough. I even thought that he was proud of me.

On the evening itself, though, he had seemed uncomfortable as though he felt out-of-place. There were so many good-looking men in suits and dark glasses, that I thought he had fit in perfectly. Perhaps that is a flippant observation. I felt a little disappointed, I must admit. My world was visual and his was visually impaired. That was the first time in my life, that I had wished to be something other than an artist. In order to have him, I would have given up my painting and gone to work in an office. I would have accepted grey.

The night of the opening, we had made love with great passion. We were happy on red wine and the excitement of the evening. Suddenly he began to sniff at me. It repulsed me and made me ache for him. Yearn for him. It began slowly. Delicate trailing of his fingers over my body. Then it became rougher. He licked me and sniffed at me, and pawed at me like a dog. Like a wild dog.

The following day as I was getting out of the shower, the telephone rang. It was Grant. He told me he didn't think we should continue the relationship. That's what he had called it. *The relationship!* It had sounded so cold. So matter-of-fact and businesslike. I was devastated. I felt used and dirty. Thrown away. I asked him why and he just said goodbye and put the phone down on me. I thought about ringing him back. Instead, I sat all day trying to understand why he had done this. At first, I wondered if there was something wrong with me, then I thought it might have been about sex. I thought it had been amazing.

It is always a blow to be rejected, to be thought not good enough. But, to be rejected by a man who cannot see. Yes, I had been falling in love with him. And now I felt hurt and stupid and angry. I had made sacrifices. I had altered my life to accept him into it and it had not been appreciated. I was shocked to see the way that my mind was working. Shocked to realise that I was the kind of person who thought that a blind man should have been grateful for the chance of being with me. I cried with exasperation and disappointment at my own failings.

Gradually, I understood that his blindness had nothing to do with the way I felt. The way he had done things had been cruel and heartless. He was not a good person, not the one for me. Another mistake. A man capable of leaving me by telephone and not explaining the reason. A man who left me in the dark, wondering what I had done wrong. Like the friends who suddenly disappear and leave you wondering why. Wondering what you did to deserve it.

If they don't want you, they don't deserve you! My old friend, Jilly always says when I need cheering up after another man has left me. I take being *abandoned* very badly. I have issues. I've had them since my sixteenth birthday when my father left to live with a woman he had met online. He left me an enormous pineapple and coconut cream-cake in the fridge and a desperate, hysterical mother on the kitchen floor.

I try not to think about Grant. Not to dwell on what happened. But it isn't easy. I still miss him. My world without him in it has lost a little colour.

***

When my mother died, I had a dream that I was in a coffin. I woke up in a panic right up against the wall. I opened my eyes and thought I had gone blind. Ever since then I have been afraid of losing my sight. I love bright colours. I love painting. I am not an artist but I may have been one in a previous life. I usually paint squares. I find it therapeutic.

My father went away on my sixteenth birthday. It was not for good, it was a holiday. It was still upsetting but he came back. He did leave me a giant pineapple and coconut cream-cake in the fridge though. Some friends from school came and stayed, and others came round the next day and helped us eat the cake.

The part about the hysterical mother on the floor is pure invention. My mother had passed away by then. That was the mother who adopted me as a baby. She was really my grandmother.

Lobster

Alice lives alone in the old town, near the fountain. The neighbourhood kids think she's crazy because she never goes out. Nobody ever goes to visit her. Her husband shot himself a long time ago. Her four children haven't forgotten her. They take it in turns to invite her for Christmas. The youngest daughter, Emma, phones her once a week, unless she's busy.

Alice isn't old but she doesn't look after herself. Loneliness ages you if you let it. She looks like the body she's wearing is a size too big. It's a bit baggy here and there. Her breasts are shrivelled. More like prunes than melons. She can never find a bra that fits and she wears big black blouses to cover her fat stomach. When she puts the rubbish out, Alice often worries that if she is not quick, they will throw her in the lorry and take her away too.

She has never managed to forgive her husband for shooting himself in the car. It was their only asset. The house belongs to the council. This winter she'll struggle again to pay the bills. She has one bath a month, on the 1st, and eats bread and jam and cups of tea with condensed milk in. Her children grimace at the thought of it. Sometimes she steals from the shop at the end of the road. Raffy has seen her but he pretends he hasn't. When she goes in, he often has to *pop out back* for something. He is a kind man.

Alice's hair is usually long, though she sometimes takes the scissors to it. She dyes it every few months with a packet colour from the supermarket in town then pretends that it is natural. She says she's going grey. She has been *going grey* for twenty years or more. Alice has a difficult life but she has nice legs.

In her youth, she won *Miss Best Legs* at a holiday camp on the west coast. She had strutted up and down in her pink bikini and silver heels showing off her winner's sash. She had gone backstage before the competition with the Honourable member for Thorwell East. Behind a curtain for a *quick feel*. He'd said he wouldn't hurt her. He had lied. She'd pleaded with him that she was a virgin. She'd lied too.

When she had come out from behind the curtain, the girl in the blue polka dot bikini had gone in. The member was not honourable at all. But she'd won a cheque for £10 and dinner for four at the Blue Oyster Lounge. It had been worth having the honourable's member between her legs to see her folks eat lobster thermidor and drink champagne. It had been nice to see her father smile with pride. He would not have been proud had he only known the truth.

The wedding had to be arranged in a hurry. Curled up sandwiches and sausage rolls. Aunty Edith had made a sherry trifle with flaked almonds on the top. Jimmy had looked handsome in his brother's suit. Her mother had said he should have had a haircut.

After their first child, born very premature but surprisingly large, they'd had three more in quick succession and Jimmy had been so proud. He was a grafter and had always provided for them. The girls loved their daddy and he was in awe of the way Alice managed to make their money go so far.

He had found out quite by chance that he couldn't have children. Alice had been surprised when he shot himself. She thought that everyone knew she had been running a respectable establishment while Jimmy was down the mines.

***

I think this story is a mix of many things. I was once encouraged by my friends to enter an improvised competition for the best legs in a nightclub. I was an extremely shy teenager and declined. The prize was a bottle of champagne, if I remember well. There were no judges. It was just based on applause.

I had a friend who used to enter beauty competitions. I often went with her to put on her fake tan and baby lotion. Again, I was once asked to participate. I declined. It is always nice to be asked though.

I read about a woman whose husband had shot himself in their brand new car. I have no idea who she was and what became of her. I do love trifle and lobster.

My friend Martine, who is a chef, cooked me scampi thermidor last Good Friday and it was delicious. We sat outside on her Arabic terrace here in the oldest part of Tursi, La Rabattana. It was warm then but not as hot as it has been this summer in the South of Italy. We had other fish dishes too. I don't usually eat fish but they were good. This was part of her tradition of eating fish on Good Friday as her father had always wanted them to do. I like the way we keep the memory of our loved ones alive in the traditions that we uphold in their honour. At the end of the meal, we had lemon posset. It was divine.

Mamma

My mother-in-law said we should have stayed together for the children. I think she spelt that a-p-p-e-a-r-a-n-c-e-s. Of course, she didn't have a clue about what was going on in our marriage. She didn't know the first thing about life at home with her son. She didn't know about the cocaine or the young girls he took into his office. His secretary was used to discreetly taking long lunch breaks and she loved the designer silk neck-scarves and handbags my husband bought to pay for her silence. She could never have afforded them on what he paid her. She looked at me with pity but it was misplaced.

I hadn't slept with George for years. We had separate bedrooms on different floors. And while he was paying for cheap thrills, I was having it away with our Italian gardener. I know. It's such a cliché but I couldn't resist that sexy accent and his tight bum.

He is besotted. He doesn't seem to mind my flat chest or my skinny hips. He says he likes the way I smell. He sniffs my underwear after he has removed it. I find it embarrassing and squirm but it really turns me on. When we make love he whispers sweet somethings that I don't understand in my ear. Italian really is the language of love. *Amore, amore, amoreeee!* He shouts when we climax again and again, and again. I had never heard of multiple orgasms, let alone had them.

Now that the children are away at their father's at the weekends, we are free to live and love openly. We spend much of the time in bed. Giovanni walks around the house naked. His stomach muscles are amazing. He is a brilliant chef. I hug him from behind and rub myself against him as he prepares delicious dishes for mc. He feeds me *bucatini alla siciliana* and licks the sauce from my lips.

We're in bed. It's raining and our boxer-cross, Basil, is flat on his back in his basket, legs straight up in the air, snoring softly. As I cuddle up to Giovanni's back, I am suddenly hit by a powerful wave of happiness. I am happy. For the first time ever, I am truly happy. I feel blessed. Life is glorious.

My phone rings. It is my brother, John. When they say that life can change in a moment. That was it. I'll never forget how I felt. The phone was suddenly heavy in my hand. I remember taking a sharp breath in but I don't remember letting it out again. I don't think I ever have completely.

My grandmother's antique clock ticking in the hall seemed to be in sync with the rain falling heavily from the trees onto the decking outside. Everything was in slow motion.

I heard myself ask my brother if our mother was dead and I heard him answer that she was still alive but to get there quickly. I couldn't reply. The adrenalin burning my arms was now gripping my throat. As I drove to the hospital in the rain, my mind left my body and began to revisit the past.

I saw myself in the the little white house on the hill where we had been happy. I was a child again. I was with John and Mamma and Papà in the house where we had grown up. In Santa Vittoria. It was early afternoon and the breeze coming up from the sea was making Nonna's bougainvillea sway as though it were dancing to music that we couldn't hear. All we heard were the cicadas in the trees and the cries of the children playing in the fields.

It was Mamma's birthday and she and Nonna were laying the table. There were great platters of salami and Tuscan roast ham in a pepper crust. The fresh focaccia bread was cut roughly into pieces and served still warm on its waxy white paper wrapping. Dishes and plates of all colours and sizes, which had been in the family for as long as anyone could remember, were brimming over with delicious fare. There were glistening green olives with fennel seeds and garlic, cold yellow and red roasted peppers. There were bright sun-dried tomatoes and pickled artichoke hearts so perfect in their form, each one a work of art. There were huge plates of sliced fresh tomatoes and mozzarella di buffalo, dripping white and creamy.

It was a simple meal. It was the way the Nonni liked to eat. It was the way Mamma liked to celebrate her birthday. All the family together and any neighbours who happened to pass by. *The more the merry*, my Italian grandfather would say in his funny English as he opened flasks of red wine and called to the children to come and eat. Later there would be grappa and Nonno's limoncello made from the great waxy lemons that hung low and heavy and plentiful on the trees at the bottom of the garden.

The conversation and the laughter flowed as easily as the wine and the sounds of happy voices were blown away on the breeze to greet Zio Antonio who was coming up the road from the *pasticceria* with trays of cream-filled choux buns and a huge birthday cake for Mamma. The old-fashioned icing and the gold card around it always made John and me laugh, but Mamma was happy then. She was dancing with Papà.

How much we loved her. We were children and she was our world. Tanned and glowing from long days on the beach, her green eyes sparkling like huge emeralds, Mamma wearing her best pale blue dress. Mamma dancing to old Italian songs on the radio. Her slice of cake in one hand, a glass of wine in the other. I remember those days. I remember my father's face as he looked at her. His dark eyes brimming with what he called *happy tears*.

And always my father would scoop my brother up into his strong arms and say, *let's not forget the birthday boy*. And John would be angry and try to wriggle free. It was not his birthday until the following day. Poor John. His birthday was always overshadowed by Mamma's party. He didn't mind. He was a quiet boy.

The following day we would celebrate again in any case. Nonno would cook great big pizzas in the wood oven and the village children would peddle up the hill on their bikes; some still newish-looking, just a little scratched and chipped, others rusty and ready for a coat of paint. But it didn't matter to them. As long as they worked, it wasn't important. When their bellies were full of pizza and cake and they had all sung *tanti auguri* to John, they would freewheel back into the village.

John wouldn't show it but he was happy too. John with his grumpy expression. John who never smiled. Mamma saying, *smile John*, trying to take a happy picture to keep. John, tall and dark and quiet. John who knew the answers before Google came along. John who loved to lie in the long grass and stare at the sky.

It was John who came towards me now. His arms around me tight as I cried into the shoulder of his grey t-shirt. He didn't need to say anything. I knew that she was gone. We are alone in a faded green and white corridor. When we pull apart, I ask him how. His eyes flicker with so much pain and I know that my mother has succeeded after many failed attempts. It was her wish.

***

When I came to Italy, I lived for a short while with an English girl who worked for a dentist. I was lucky enough to spend some time with him and his family in their house in the country. It was the first time I had enjoyed the Italian outdoors and big family celebrations here. I remember thinking that I would have loved to still have that kind of family life. Some of my happiest memories are of all the family together sharing a meal, albeit in Lancashire and not in sunny Italy.

None of my three mothers took their own lives, though my adopted mother did not take care of herself well and did very little to combat her decline into a life spent in bed or in her rocking chair. Though we never got on, I wish that she had taken more care of her health. Watching her die slowly was difficult for me. It must have been difficult for her too. After she passed, my boxer dog used to look at the rocking chair. I wondered if he was wondering why she wasn't in it anymore.

We never spoke about my mother again. There were no pictures of her on display. It was almost as if she had never been there. I found that very sad.

The Last Resort

Why her husband had thought that the south-west coast of England would be full of empty bed and breakfast establishments at the end of August was beyond her. She was a planner and he was, well, not a planner. They had spent the entire day driving from place to place looking for a vacancies sign.

Her stomach was grumbling. Wilf did not want them to eat anything between breakfast and their evening meal, and she had an enormous blister on her right heel. It had burst and was stinging like crazy, as they trailed from place to place. Her head was spinning and her throat was parched. She was quickly losing her patience with Wilf and then, an apparition! *Vacancies.* A white house on the coast with one free room at the very top. A short walk to the beach. A quaint-looking pub not far away. A cooked breakfast included. Perfection at a salty price.

Wilf parked the car and unloaded their luggage. He huffed and puffed as he carried two heavy suitcases and several bags up the four flights of stairs to the loft conversion that was to be their home for the next two weeks. It was hot.

They walked to the pub and ordered scampi, which arrived breaded and in a basket. Wilf kissed her across the table. She shuffled uncomfortably on the bench-type seat that she had clambered over in order to sit down. It had not been lady-like in a white summer skirt with a spattering of pink roses.

Wilf sucked the salt from her lips and kissed her wrists and the palms of her hands. She told him to behave himself. There were people watching. Wilf did not care. He said that he would give them something to watch. He frightened her when he had been drinking. He was not a violent drunk as such but he was unpredictable. She was always on guard on evenings like this.

There was an elderly man at the bar in a navy blazer. Bushy greyish white hair and beard. He looked like a sea captain. Perhaps the bar paid him for his services. He was singing songs in a language she'd never heard. She thought it might be Cornish. At the end of each song he would belt out a hearty laugh and shout, 'oh yeah!' A bizarre character who added a little life to the quiet pub.

Wilf found him amusing and began to laugh and applaud him. She laughed too, trying to enjoy the evening. Wilf ordered more drinks. She felt that she had had enough already. She had an uneasy feeling in her stomach. She wished he would stop drinking. This was no longer fun. His hands on her wrists were a little tighter now. She tried to pull away.

She pretended to feel unwell and told Wilf that she would walk back to the B&B and see him there later. He seemed angry, willing her to stay and enjoy the evening. But she was adamant. She hoped he wouldn't risk causing a scene here.

Out in the fresh black air of the night, she breathed deeply. The night was cool and still and silent. She set off to walk along the seafront, back to the white house. She didn't see him follow her out of the pub. She didn't hear him walking some distance behind her. Didn't realise that she was in danger.

When his hands closed in around her throat, she fought. She kicked and struggled for all she was worth, as though her life depended on it. It did. But he was strong and big. She brought her knee up to wind him, as she knew you should, but was not quick enough. When her head hit the pavement, she could move no more. She lay, semi-conscious as he pulled up her skirt. She lay semi-conscious with tears rolling down her face as he thrust himself upon her. She saw his eyes and remembered his face as he rolled her under the railings and down the steep wall to the sea.

The water was cold and salty, and dark and smelly. The waves were fierce, and angry and unforgiving. She disappeared into the black sea, going under and reappearing several times before she resurfaced no more. Her body was never recovered. The last thing she thought before her life left her was that she should have stayed in the pub with her husband. She had loved him.

***

This story is based on a holiday I took with my, then, new husband. I was indeed irritated that he had refused to book accommodation and exasperated at spending our days trailing around looking for a place to stay. I was not, obviously, killed; though we did have some very strange experiences on our holidays in the UK.

Once we knocked on the front door of a B&B and were greeted by a woman reminiscent of Morticia Addams. The tall, slim lady in a very tight purple dress with flowing sleeves, took us up several floors of her ancient and very dark house to look at the room. We were not impressed. She then told us where to park the car and to go around to the front door. When we went to look for the front door, we could no longer find the number. I am very embarrassed to say that we just drove off and looked for somewhere else.

The *somewhere else* was run by a very nice lady. There was a crucifix above the bed and a few bedsprings sticking out of it. The next morning, the breakfast would have been almost edible had it not been for the addition of one very large tinned plum tomato, complete with watery juice. Perhaps we should have searched a little harder for *Morticia*.

In the Stars

My brother has a new girlfriend. Her name is Amanda. She's slim and blonde and bubbly and I can tell he really likes her. They stay in his room listening to music. I know they're not really listening to music and I think Mum knows too. When they come out, their faces are a bit red and their hair is messed up. She has blue eyes and is a Gemini. I think she's really pretty. I am so jealous of my brother. I wish that she was mine. *Thou shalt not covet thy brother's girlfriend!*

But I do covet her. I covet her all the time. My brother is a Virgo and I really don't think they're well suited. My brother is so methodical and analytical. I find Amanda's natural creativity stifled by him. She is a dancer. Her body is so supple. I go to watch her sometimes. I hide behind a pillar. I see her during preparation when she is stretching. She can stand on one leg and arch the other over her head. She is so fluid in her movements, so flowingly *unrigid* and unmethodical. She is a free spirit. I shall spirit her away from my brother. I shall make this my goal.

I am a Libra. I like harmony, peace and justice. It is not very *just* to steal my brother's girlfriend. It will not create *harmony* but war. I am intelligent and persuasive. I know I can entice her away. I am an air-sign. I am agreeable and honest. It is neither *agreeable* nor *honest* to try to steal my brother's girlfriend.

I have weighed up the advantages and the disadvantages. I am a Libra. I can see all sides of an argument. It is a blessing and a curse. The disadvantage is that my brother will be angry and vindictive. He is a Virgo. He will not forgive me. The advantage is that I will be with Amanda. I will be the one to touch Amanda. To kiss Amanda. To embrace Amanda. I am a Libra. In case you have not noticed, I am a little self-absorbed.

I know my brother is making plans for their life together. He is a Virgo. He has his future all mapped out. I know that he will stifle Amanda with his perfectly ordered existence. I must act fast before he snares her in his trap. Luckily, he is not one to take things quickly. He is still thinking things through. He likes to be prepared.

Gemini and Virgo is not the best match. They have already started to bicker and disagree. My brother is quiet and pensive. He is floored by Amanda's impulsivity. He doesn't like surprises.

I begin to flirt with Amanda and she responds playfully. My brother is put out but tries not to show it. We become good friends. I ask her if she wants to come to a party with me one night when I know my brother has other plans. She accepts.

The party is the perfect occasion to make my move. We chat all evening and dance. We toast each other with paper cups of cheap red wine. I reach in to kiss her. I push my hands under her sweater and cup her breasts. I have never kissed a girl before and neither has she. She is surprised and tells me that she has always been very attracted to me, she just didn't ever think of herself as being with a woman, a girl.

Our romance is a whirlwind of parties and socializing and sex. We cannot get enough of each other. Sparks fly between us. I love her body and she loves mine. We are similar in shape but she is slimmer. More supple. The way she moves when we make love fascinates me.

My brother is angry. He stops talking to me. He is hurt although he hides it. I feel a slight sense of shame and of loss. I know that he will never speak to me again. But I have Amanda. She is worth it.

A couple of weeks after we got together, Amanda met Sabrina. Sabrina is a Leo. They are the perfect match. Sabrina likes fuchsia pinks and turquoises and wears her red hair loose like a mane. She drives a battered car that has passed its test, but she is not sure how. She cooks every day with passion and with patience. She is creative. She is kind. Her heart is big. I can see why Amanda adores her. I think I adore her too.

Libra and Leo is not the best match. I think the sex and the passion will be great but will not last. I do not want to hurt Amanda but I am so attracted to Sabrina. We have started to go out all together. Two is company, three is not a crowd when we are together. Three is the perfect number. The perfect combination of limbs and mouths and fingers.

Sabrina is a generous lover. She is so elegant and chic. We are drawn to each other's beauty. Our relationship is not just sexual. There is more to it. We go out often. We have become *the party girls*. We talk a lot too. Sabrina listens carefully. She is not often quiet. She is a ball of energy bouncing between us. She thinks everything happens for a reason and accepts the situation. She is the leader of the three. She craves our adoration. Our union is not typical or traditional but it works. I cannot find anything online to tell me if Libra, Gemini and Leo are a compatible match, but I know that we are perfect together.

We move into a house in the country, away from prying eyes. We get two rescue dogs and grow our own tomatoes. We are happy.

***

One day, on the beach with Martine, we began talking about star signs. I have never really believed much in them until I read my own and

Martine's and found that they were incredibly precise. I then read about how compatible we were as friends and was blown away when it said that Leos could encourage Libras to follow their dreams. Martine is the person who encouraged me to write my first collection of stories. Many others had done so before, but this Libra needed a Leo to make her do it.

The rest of the story is complete fiction. I am a very quiet person who stays at home happily writing and enjoying the company of her Labrador and Martine has a long-term partner. He is a lovely man.

In any case, it really doesn't matter. Love is love.

The Cork

I love telling people about how I first met my husband on a train. It's such a romantic story. I was on my own, travelling from the Italian Riviera to the South of France to meet my father. It was one of those rickety old trains with carriages where you all sit together, and I found myself sitting next to a very good-looking Italian boy. Between Rapallo, where I had been staying, and Bordighera where my Italian boy got off the train, there are a surprising number of tunnels and, as the lights in our carriage were not working, we remained in darkness for a time every now and then. It rather reminded me of the Orient Express. Not that I have ever been on the Orient Express. But, instead of being murdered, I was kissed! Yes, every time we went through a tunnel, the boy kissed me on the cheek and every time we came out of the tunnel, he sat there all innocent as though nothing had happened.

I wasn't sure whether to be shocked or flattered. My instinct was to laugh. As we reached the third tunnel, I made up my mind, and turned and kissed him back, putting my hand on his knee. As we came out of the tunnel, it was his turn to be dumbfounded and, as I sat looking straight ahead, innocently, I saw from the corner of my eye a smile break out on his face. He really was quite handsome. Thus we spent the rest of our journey kissing passionately in every tunnel, my hand going further and further up his leg until I reached a point where he let out a little moan and didn't manage to look quite as composed when we came back out into bright sunshine. The two elderly ladies in front of us were making it clear that they were not amused.

When we reached Bordighera and my Italian boy got off the train, he tore the front page from the book he had been pretending to read and held the train up whilst he wrote his name and address for me. On the remaining part of the page, he asked me to write mine. His name was Mattia Ferrari. The name sounded familiar. I thought it might be just the racing car that I was thinking of, but then something occurred to me. I looked at the cork in the pocket of my bag. The name on it was, *Ferrari*. He was the one. My destiny. I had found my Italian love. Better late than never!

I had been helping out at a bar in Rapallo for the summer before I started university. The owner, Elena, was an old friend of my mother. My three months in Italy had flown by in a haze of collecting and washing glasses and cleaning tables, mopping floors and filling bowls of crisps and nuts. I only worked part-time and Elena was very good to me. She gave me a beautiful little apartment at the top of the building. Four floors of steps, but the climb was worth it. It was a small room with an old cooker and a huge ceramic sink and a sofa-come-bed in the corner. The bathroom was old too, but it was clean. It was my first experience of living alone.

I had been excited to spend my first night in my new home. Then, in the morning when I'd opened the windows and the heavy green shutters, I'd cried. I had my own little balcony with a tiny round marble-topped table and two wrought iron chairs. And the most amazing view I'd ever seen. I shall never forget sitting there, looking out across the palm-tree-lined road and the promenade at the sea sparkling silver and bright in the morning sun. I sat and stared while my coffee went cold. My little piece of paradise. I felt my heart swell with anticipation of my adventure. I was free. I was young. I was in Italy.

I was intent on making as many special memories as I could before I went back to England and I did. I was eighteen and in love with life. I soon fell in love with Italy too. I adored the sea, the blue skies, the sunrises, the food, the people, and the crazy traffic. Everything. I felt like I was floating. The smile that spread across my face could not be controlled. Wherever I went, people would call out to me, *Buongiorno bella inglesina!* And I would feel a warm glow that they all thought of me as *the beautiful little English girl*.

In my free time, and Elena made sure that I had a lot of it, I walked and walked for miles. I went out on boat trips and saw amazing coves and tiny little fishing villages with coloured boats, and coloured houses climbing up the hills. I ate spaghetti and *focaccia di Recco* (two very thin layers of crisp unrisen flakey focaccia with a delicious liquidy, cheesy filling). The most heavenly thing I had ever eaten. That was until I tried real Ligurian pesto. I was in food heaven. Elena introduced me to bruschetta and *pansotti* (herby pasta parcels which were served with a creamy walnut sauce), and delicious fish dishes.

I was, of course, putting on a little weight but I was getting fit with all the walking and Elena said I was too thin and a few extra kilos suited me. I had arrived in Italy a pale, skinny girl and I felt like I was turning into a tanned and glowing young woman. That probably sounds bigheaded. But that is how I felt. For the first time in my life, I stopped feeling invisible and started to have some confidence in my looks.

Elena helped me to choose the right clothes and accessories at the Thursday market or in the numerous little boutique shops. The Italians are so stylish. I know it's frivolous, but it made me happy. She took me to her hairdresser and taught me how to apply my make-up. I didn't wear much, it was so hot. I always managed to lick the lipstick away as I was forever eating.

On the one hand, I wanted to stay here forever, but I was missing Mum and Dad and I was looking forward to starting university and showing off my tan and my new wardrobe. When I left, I had two heavy cases packed with clothes and bags and shoes and, of course, presents for my family and friends. I had bought silk scarves for my mother and my aunt, a beautiful leather bag for my sister and sunglasses and silver jewellery from the Senegalese and Mauritian street sellers near the sea. For Dad, Elena had recommended a bottle of wine. Thank goodness he would be picking me up in France and driving me back home. He had arranged to be in Cannes on business.

My time in Italy was coming to an end. I had climbed hills and gazed at sunsets. I had walked miles along little pathways, marvelling at the tiny lizards darting in and out of crevices in dry stone walls. I had swum in the sea and eaten ice cream in beautiful piazzas – pistachio, *lampone*, even cheesecake flavour. I had borrowed a scooter from Elena's daughter and zig-zagged through traffic then up winding hills and quiet roads, stopping to take in views out over the olive groves and down to the blue, blue sea.

I had danced to music that sounded exotic to my ears when bands had come to play in the square on *festa* nights. I had seen firework displays and eaten freshly caught fish. I was in love with my life in Italy. But one thing had been missing. I had secretly hoped that I would meet somebody special and have a summer romance but it was not to be. Some of the customers had flirted with me and I had turned a few heads, but I was shy and nobody had asked me out. Perhaps it had been for the best. I had enjoyed my days exploring alone.

On my last night at the bar, Elena made snacks and ordered a cake from the *pasticceria* across the road. She popped the cork on a bottle of *spumante* and made a toast to my safe journey to

England and my speedy return to Italy. She took the cork and pressed a coin into the top of it, saying that if I kept it, I would come back again one day. It was a lovely sentiment and I adored Elena, but I did not think I would see her again. It had been an amazing three months but my future was in England. I couldn't wait to start university. I was eager to stand on my own two feet.

The next morning, with the cork in the pocket of my bag for good luck, I set off from the little train station. Elena's brother had to go with me to put my cases on the overhead racks. I hugged them both and said my goodbyes. I would miss them and I would miss my little balcony overlooking the sea but I was eager to see my family. I waved until I could no longer see them.

It was wonderful to arrive in France and be met by my father. I always have been a Daddy's girl. He was looking tanned and relaxed, despite his business meetings. We stayed overnight in a little guest house near the sea.

We ate *moules marinières* at a lovely bistro. I rarely get the chance to have dinner alone with my father. It was lovely to relax and tell him all about my time in Italy and to listen to him telling me what had been happening at home in my absence. I think that was one of my happiest times with him.

Back home in the UK, I spent some time with my family and then started packing for university. One morning, my mother told me that there was a letter for me from Italy. On the back of the letter was the name and address. It was from Mattia. He had written to me in English. I eagerly read his news. Then I took my Italian dictionary and began to write a reply. It was painstakingly slow and I had no idea if my Italian was comprehensible, but I did it.

Mattia replied, again in English, and thus began our correspondence over the autumn and winter months. I would tell him about my life at university in England and he would tell me about his life at university in Italy. We talked about our families, our friends, our interests. My Italian became more fluent, though I imagine that it was full of mistakes. My feelings towards Mattia were blossoming into something important. I kept the cork that Elena had given me on my bedside table and held it often. *Ferrari*. He was the one. I was sure that it was our destiny to be together.

The following spring, Elena asked me to go back to work in the bar and I jumped at the chance. I couldn't wait to see her and my friends, but most of all I wanted to see Mattia. My father was not impressed at me taking time out of university, but I was an adult and, in any case, it would only be a few weeks added on to the Easter break.

I booked my flight and waited eagerly for the day to arrive. Elena said she would send her brother to meet me at the airport in Genoa, but I said he didn't need to. Mattia said he would be there and he was. He was just as handsome as I remembered him. I could feel the butterflies in my stomach fluttering excitedly.

I fell into his arms and hugged him close, my love, my destiny. I was so happy and, to my amazement, Mattia seemed to feel the same way. He drove me to Elena's bar and waited for me while I quickly put my case in my little room and freshened up. Then, we went down to spend the evening in the bar with Elena and her family.

As usual, Elena was so happy to see me and threw a party in my honour. As she popped the cork on the spumante and turned up the music, she danced and laughed. I held Mattia's hand under the table and felt like I would burst with happiness. I couldn't wait to spend some time with him and get to know him in person rather than in writing.

Elena filled our glasses and handed me a cork with a coin in the top. It was not the one from the bottle she had just opened. I looked at her quizzically. 'The cork I gave you last time was the wrong one.' She held her hand to her forehead in a gesture meaning *sorry* and apologized. 'This is the right cork but it doesn't matter. You came back even with the wrong cork,' she laughed. I looked down at the cork in my hand and read the surname *Giorgi* on the top.

***

My Facebook friend, Michele, gave me the idea for this story. She sent me just a few words and told me to do with them as I wished. She met her husband on a train. (I am quite sure she did not kiss him passionately in any tunnels nor feel his thighs!) His surname turned out to be on the top of a cork that she had been given before she came to Italy. The surnames on the top of corks, either belong to the makers or the place where *spumante* is made in Italy. The name on Michele's cork was not very common at all.

The rest of this story is fiction, though it is based on my knowledge of the area around Rapallo in Liguria on the Italian Riviera. I lived in and around that area for many years before moving south. It is truly beautiful.

I hope Michele likes what I have done with her story.

Footprints

He'd been through this twice already with the older girls and now it was Sophie's turn. Suddenly they were there like wasps around a fig tree returning, over and over, trying to suck the pink sticky juice.

He tried not to go out at night. Not to leave her on her own. But sometimes he had no choice. Her mother had left them and her sisters were married off. Sophie was all he had. His pride and his joy. His sunshine. He had tried but he had failed her.

That night in February, he had been called out to a van stuck at the bottom of the road. He didn't think he would be long but the driver had offered him a drink to thank him and, stupidly, he had nipped into the Wagon and Horses for a quick pint and a tot of rum to warm himself up. Several glasses of rum later, he had staggered up the hill, his legs flying out from under him in the heavy snow.

When he got home she was quiet. Flushed. It had happened. He knew it was too late to punish her. He knew he should be punishing someone else – and he would. Oh, he would.

He took his belt off to her. She didn't flinch. She was a proud child. Only fourteen. A beauty. The prettiest of his girls. The eldest had the brains and the youngest the attitude but his Sophie had the looks. A sweet child like her mother and, like her mother, she had the curves and the blue eyes.

His name is Rick. A lanky piece of shite. It took a while to get him on his own. The police report on the news said he had been dragged down a pathway into the park, after dark by four men who had beaten him around the head and the genitals with heavy objects. He had a broken jaw and black eyes and they had to operate on him twice.

Years later, when she was a young woman with children of her own, Sophie had asked her father how he had known about the boy that she had invited into the house. *There were footprints in the snow*, he'd said.

Rick recovered slowly from surgery but he would never be the same. He couldn't get an erection any longer. His penis lay flaccid. A useless appendage. His jaw healed but his spirit didn't. The blows to his head had damaged his brain. He had always been bad but now he was evil.

He took to hiding in the trees and spying on couples having sex. He thought that might help him but it didn't. He felt even more frustrated. He started to think about how it would feel to get his hands around a girl's throat and squeeze the life out of her. Women were whores and he wanted them to pay.

Bill and his daughter had already moved to Milton Keynes when a spate of killings were reported in the park near where they used to live.

***

After my first mother passed away, my father was often out working or looking for another wife, so I was alone, except for my boxer dog. I had a very strict upbringing. I don't remember my father ever saying that I wasn't to let anyone in at night, but I knew that I shouldn't. My own mother (the daughter of the man I called Dad), had got pregnant with me at just eighteen and I think he was worried about the same thing happening to me.

One night two boys that I knew from along the road came to my house and asked to come in. I kept telling them *no*, but they were in t-shirts and it was snowing. In the end, I let them in. They only stayed for tea but I realised that I had put myself in danger. When my father arrived home and saw the footprints in the snow, I was in trouble, again.

The older I get, the sadder and angrier I am to think that we women cannot enjoy our lives and our friendships and our experiences without forever having to think that men could pose a threat to us.

I have just returned from a trip to a seaside town. It was low season and there were not many tourists around, but it was most certainly not deserted. In fact, after spending six months in a hilltop hamlet, I was rather shocked at just how many people there were!

On my birthday, as I walked back to my hotel after having had lunch with my son, a man asked me if I wanted a lift. He commented on how far I had walked. It was afternoon and there were other people and lots of traffic. I realised that he had been walking behind me and must have been doing so for some time. I was sitting on a bench and had to reach for my phone and pretend to call somebody.

The man left and I thought no more of it until, as I continued to walk towards my hotel, I found him waiting for me. It was by then, just starting to get dark. I walked along a cycle path where there were lots of people but I felt uncomfortable and kept checking that he was not following me. He wasn't.

It saddens me to think that all girls and women have had to deal with similar situations.

The Big Day

'Yes to the peacocks, no to the Chinese lanterns.' Lucy thought they were dangerous. She could just imagine one floating off and setting the awnings of the venue alight and their wedding ending up on the news. Peacocks, on the other hand, seemed to be quite sweet and gentle birds. They would bring a touch of class to their special day. She was sure of it.

'A definite no to the wedding cake with marzipan flowers.' She wondered if there was a single person in the world who actually liked marzipan. And, it was so very heavy. Not at all the thing to have at the end of a sixteen-course meal. She wanted something light after the strawberries and ice cream. They settled on the *millefoglie*, a French cake made from layers of Chantilly cream and flaky pastry. She was not sure how they would make it into a wedding cake but that was their problem. She was tired.

'Yes to the chocolate fountain!' It was all going to be so chic. She could just imagine the ten little bridesmaids in their powder pink dresses, dipping marshmallows on sticks into the flowing chocolate.

The wedding planner stopped to tie his shoelace, his foot resting rudely on the edge of the swimming pool. Lucy and Martin waited for him to continue the tour of the venue. She really wanted to see where the welcome cocktail would be served, and needed to check out the rooms where their families and friends would be staying when they arrived from Wales.

She turned to see that Martin had wandered off to look at the view. He was always so distracted these days. If only her mother could have been convinced to come over sooner. They could have done all this without him. He did not seem in the least bit interested in anything. He had no opinion on the cake, the flowers, or the food. He didn't seem to give a fig, and was more than happy to go with the flow. That was fine by her, as she liked to take control of the situation. She wanted everything just so. But, a little more enthusiasm would not go amiss.

Lucy's stomach growled. Two weeks to go until the wedding and she still needed to lose half a stone. She took a sip of water from the bottle in her bag. Martin came up behind her and wrapped his arms around her, 'Babe, let's eat here. I'm starving!' At last, he has expressed a desire, she thought. Such a pity that it was connected to his stomach and not to the wedding. But, it would be a good idea to try the food out again. The last time, on the day they'd found and booked the venue, it had been exceptional. But things change.

Martin was always hungry and always eating, yet he never seemed to put on weight. She loved the fact that he was tall and slim. She loved the way her girl friends eyed him up. He was a hunk and she knew that she was lucky. But she didn't want him to make her look short and dumpy on her wedding photos. They would have to be photoshopped.

The wedding planner took them quickly around the rooms. They were fresh and white and nearly all of them had a sea view. Lucy was sure her family and friends would love them. She couldn't wait for her mother to arrive. She wanted to share everything with her, and not just by telephone.

Then they checked the menu one last time; yes, she really did want seven antipasti! The wedding planner took a few photos to show their own photographer and the florist, and got back into his black Porsche, waving through the open window as he zoomed away. Lucy and Martin went happily back up the steps to the restaurant.

Obviously, it was mostly fish, being this close to the sea. She thought they might have a mixed salad or something light. The waiter looked unperturbed. He said he would ask the chef. He was sure that they could prepare something light. He was used to these requests. It was highly-strung-bride-wanting-to-lose-weight-for-the-wedding season, and not at all unusual for him to have clients come to the restaurant but not want to eat.

Martin ordered the antipasto di mare and the pasta with prawns and zucchini. He then tucked into a huge white fish, which arrived on a trolley and was cleaned and boned in front of them. Lucy felt nauseas. He ordered fries to go with it. She crunched quietly on a lettuce leaf and looked longingly at the desserts trolley arriving for the people on the next table. She longed to eat profiteroles and cheesecake and panna cotta. She wanted steak and chips, and pasta and pizza instead of this bland salad. She was tired of dieting, and was feeling somewhat overwrought. She wished she could just take it all in her stride like Martin.

Her anxiety was getting the better of her. She really wanted to leave, but Martin had asked for *torta della nonna* from the trolley, some kind of cake. When he asked her if she wanted to try it, she (momentarily) thought of pulling a copper pan off the wall and hitting him with it. He had asked for it to be served with both ice cream and whipped cream. She wanted to be him. She wanted to stuff her face and stay slim. She must resist. A few more pounds and her wedding dress would fit like a glove instead of leaving her breathless and worried that it might burst at the seams.

The following weeks flew by in a haze of phone calls and fittings and checking endless details. They spent a few days on the beach topping up their tans. Lucy adored Italy. It would be so lovely to stay on here and honeymoon after the wedding was over. Then their family and friends started arriving and they were kept busy going to pick them up from the airport or the train station.

Finally, the big day arrived. The sun was shining. The guests were happy. The groom did not do a runner. It had never once crossed Lucy's mind that he would. The church service was short and sweet, as they had requested. The guests had applauded and then thrown their rice. The welcome drinks and nibbles were superb. The dress fit perfectly. Her father looked proud. Her mother and her three sisters were crying. All was going to plan.

They made the local newspapers and were even on TV. The article was both sad and amusing. The happy couple and their wedding guests had been on their way up the steps to start their meal after the welcome cocktail on the terrace, when they had been attacked. It was mating season and the ostentation of peacocks, roaming free in the grounds, had reacted aggressively to the fascinators, of all forms and colours, but mostly some variation on the theme of feathers, being sported by all the female wedding guests and one or two of the males.

The mother of the bride had been the first to be jumped upon and pecked at. She had fallen backwards down the steps and landed unceremoniously on the mother of the groom. In a domino-type scenario, one by one, the guests had knocked each other over and were left rolling on the lawn where they were easy prey for the furious peacocks who had now ganged up and were in full attack-mode, while the terrified guests cried out for help.

Lucy began to cry. She had really had enough now. Enough of wedding talk and weddings and *smile please* and flowers and rings and… Enough. Enough of starving to death. She had thought she could finally go and have something to eat, but no. This mess would have to be sorted out.

The warm antipasti would now be cold, the main courses, should they ever get to eat them, would be overcooked, she was distraught and Martin was just standing there as usual.

Lucy hitched up her dress and underskirts and legged it to the waiting Rolls. The driver was having a quick fag on the terrace at the back of the hotel before lunch. He wouldn't have to drive the couple to their hotel until much later. She had never driven a Rolls Royce before, but once she had backed out of the car park (only hitting a couple of cars and just grazing the wall ever so slightly), Lucy started to get the hang of it.

The staff at the Pizzeria Bella Napoli down the road were all a little surprised to see a lone bride driving a Rolls Royce arrive, but they were happy enough to serve her a giant spicy sausage pizza and a side of chips and battered onion rings, followed by two helpings of profiteroles and, not a peacock in sight.

***

I got married a long time ago in Italy in August. I loved the day itself and I loved being married. Though I normally enjoy planning things, I found wedding planning very stressful. We had neither peacocks nor chocolate fountains, though we did have *millefoglie* and it was delicious. None of my guests wore fascinators, though all the English women had hats. If I were to do it again, I would just wear a simple dress and say *yes* on the beach.

I have never stolen a Rolls Royce.

The Green Watering Can

It was a strange thing to buy someone for Christmas, especially as it was now April. You said that you had forgotten. *Forgotten?* How can you forget Christmas? Anyway, it was nice of you to bring it with you. I hadn't expected a Christmas present on our Easter holiday. Wrapped in Christmas paper too. But then, you always were a little, well, different.

I love this quiet place we've found. In the hills in Devon. The weather is amazingly warm this year. We have even swum in the sea. It took our breath away and made us gasp ha ha, but we did it. The rooms are all separate buildings with a main farmhouse where breakfast is served. Our room is enormous. The giant bed, for some reason, is in one corner. It is a long walk on the cold stone tiles to the ensuite bathroom.

One wall of the room, which must have been some kind of barn where animals were kept once over, has been removed and almost the entire wall is taken up by a glass window that slides open onto a beautiful paved terrace. Anybody could just walk by but we leave the blinds open. We don't care. We love to lay in bed and watch the sun come up over the sea.

The other days we have asked for breakfast to be served on the terrace. The couple who bring it are not English. They are young. Albanians I think they said. They tell us their names. I forget them immediately. I have never been good with names. They look like people who work hard for very little money and I feel guilty thinking of how much we have spent on this place. Yes, yes, we had a special offer. A discount.

The breakfast is good. Bread and croissants, and cereal and cake and jams and biscuits. Different teas and coffees, and juices of all descriptions. We always eat everything. We are young. We are hungry. We are also curious. At least, *you* are curious. You want to see what the breakfast is like at the farmhouse. It's fine. I don't mind. I'm washed and dressed and waiting for you on the patio, reading my book and swinging my long legs.

We really aren't one of those couples that likes to have breakfast at a long table with other people. We are more your let's-sit-alone-in-the-corner type of couple. But we are here now and you are right. There is more choice here and more food. We are asked if we would like a cooked breakfast, the famous English breakfast that we were expecting to try here. We say *yes, please* and join the other guests at the very long table.

The man sitting opposite me is cutting up the cooked breakfast for his wife. She only has one arm. At the end of the table is a great big Scottish man complete with bushy grey beard. The lady of the house brings him a steaming bowl of porridge. I hate the smell of porridge.

Just as I am thinking how very bizarre the situation is, a geisha walks into the breakfast room and stands by the side of the Scottish gentleman. Yes, a geisha! I did not know that they still existed, and wasn't expecting to find one in the UK. She is truly beautiful in full make-up and costume with her black hair looking so perfect. Perhaps it is a wig.

I am lost for words, but you, being such a gentleman, say, 'Good morning!' You are very quickly told not to talk to her and pretend that she is not there. I found the whole thing hilarious and really didn't know where to look. On reflection though, and in these different times, it is more than a little sad that a woman should stand at the side of a man while he eats his porridge and be completely ignored by the other five people in the room.

I slide my fried tomatoes onto your plate, trying not to be too obvious. I like the bacon and the sausages and egg. There are triangles of something strange, perhaps potato and baked beans. I have never tried baked beans. They seem like an odd choice for breakfast. In Italy we would probably eat beans in a soup for dinner. But they taste good. We are satisfied.

We decided to play Frisbee outside on the lawn but it was cold and windy and our fingers froze. We laughed so much we cried. I still have a photograph of you running after the Frisbee but you never got to see it.

We walked around a local town. There was a street market selling traditional cheeses and pies and jams. It was lovely but we had eaten too much. We were tempted by chocolates and cakes, but we resisted until the very end when we came upon a stall that sold only fudge. We studied all the different flavours for ages trying to understand them, then trying to decide. You had rum and raisin and I had gingerbread. I did not know exactly what it was but it tasted good. Spicy.

We had dinner at an Italian restaurant. Yes, I know. It's crazy to eat Italian food abroad but the owner told us he was from Naples and we were tired of British food and not knowing what would arrive when we ordered. We were tired of pubs and all the restaurants were Chinese or French, or Indian. There did not seem to be English restaurants. We had pizza. It was ok. We drank rather a lot of expensive red wine.

We tried to sleep either side of the broken bedspring, too tired to go down and complain. In the end, we slept. Too drunk to worry about it scratching us. We tried very hard to be a happy couple on holiday but we weren't. We both knew that.

When I woke up, you had gone. I hugged my green watering can and cried, grief-stricken that you had left me until I realised that it was a relief not to have to pretend anymore. Waiting for the end had been worse than accepting that you were gone.

The people there were kind. They called an ambulance, although we knew it was too late. They tried to bring you back to life but you were gone. It was not a shock. I had been expecting it. We had both known that there was not much time left.

I travelled back to Italy alone. Your family was arranging to join you and have you flown back. I still sleep on my side of the bed and leave your side empty for when you come back from your holidays.

They think I am crazy. They tell me you are dead but I know that can't be true. You are on holiday in England and I am here watering the plants with my green watering can and waiting for you to come back so that we can get married in summer, the way we always planned.

***

The love of my life was rather distracted. He was probably the kindest and most intelligent man I have ever met. He once bought me a green watering can for Christmas. He was not so distracted as to give it to me at Easter! He passed away suddenly. It took me a long time to believe that I would never see him again.

The Spy who Loved Him

When she married her first, indeed only, boyfriend, a certain Cecil Bond, the woman who was to become my mother took rather a funny turn. She was evermore convinced that she was a spy. *My name is Bond, Flora Bond*, she would pronounce often as she peeled potatoes at the tiny kitchen sink that looked out onto our damp yard.

My father took the whole thing well at first. He considered it a harmless jest. He had spent most of his life being ribbed about his surname. *Boys will be boys*, his father had said once.

When I was born, it looked as though my mother was recovering. Family members noticed that her behaviour was less erratic. But, when I was a little older, she went back to her old ways.

I remember when she took to following people and making notes about what they did. She followed a lady in a green coat and headscarf who was buying apples at the local green grocer's. Her notes read: Elsie, 3 granny smiths, walked home to Thurnham Street, Number 27, red door. 10.02.

When Mother followed a young dark-haired chap in a raincoat all the way along the canal banks one day, my father became alarmed and asked her to stop. For a while, she would go to the park and sit next to strangers on benches. She would pull out a newspaper and, hiding behind it, she would whisper things that made them so uncomfortable that they moved to another bench. Some of them left the park.

My father pleaded with her to stop this stuff-and-nonsense but she was unable or unwilling. She was Flora Bond, a woman on a mission. Her jaunts became more frequent and further afield. Then, one Thursday at the end of March, she was brought home by the police.

Daddy was a very private man and he was most displeased. He begged her to stop this folly. He even threatened to leave.

Spring and summer passed with relative calm. Mummy stayed at home and made meatloaf and Viennese swirls but she could be heard repeating, *My name is Bond, Flora Bond* as she added wine to the boeuf bourguignon.

In autumn, my mother had driving lessons and passed her test first time. She had been used to driving the tractors and old cars on the farm where she'd lived as a child. One day she drove to the coast doing 15 miles an hour. She was blissfully unaware that she was holding up the traffic.

She booked herself a single room at the Marlborough Arms, behind the gas works. It was a clean enough establishment and good enough for what she had in mind. The proprietor brought her a lukewarm cup of stewed tea with two pink wafers on the saucer.

At 7 pm, Flora Bond extracted a French pistol from a handkerchief in her handbag and slipped it into the pocket of her camel-coloured coat. She left the car in the car park and walked to the entrance of the Horse and Hound. She waited patiently behind, in fact slightly in, a mulberry bush. It was a cold and frosty evening.

As the happy couple came out of the pub laughing and joking, their arms wrapped around each other, my mother followed them down the street. Her hand still clutching the pistol in her pocket. When the road was quiet enough, she stepped out right behind them and pointed the gun. 'My name is Bond. Flora Bond,' she cried as the alarmed couple raised their hands.

Ignoring their gesture of surrender, my mother tried to shoot them both and, despite the short distance between them, managed somehow to miss. The police were called posthaste.

I take the number 38 bus once a week to see my mother. She is not in prison yet but has been detained in a mental institution awaiting trial. She is rapidly losing weight and looks rather gaunt. The medication has finally made her forget that she is a spy.

Some years later, my father remarried. His new wife is a nurse with a gap between her front teeth. A lovely lady who keeps Yorkshire Terriers. She doesn't go out of the house as she is afraid of getting shot after an unfortunate incident with a lady in a camel-coloured coat.

***

I have no idea where this story sprang from. I doubt very much that any of my three mothers were spies, nor, as far as I know, did they ever think they were. None of them ever tried to shoot anyone. Only one of them drove. Though I never saw her in a camel-coloured coat. That is not to say that she never had one.

My third mother, or rather, the woman my grandfather married when his wife, (my grandmother and adopted mother – yes, I know it's complicated, sorry) passed away, was a retired nurse and had two Yorkshire Terriers. She didn't have a gap between her teeth and was often to be seen outside of the house.

I moved into my stepmother's house and lived with them for a short while. I didn't like my bedroom much. I was going through a phase of being punk. I wanted to dye my hair pink but my father wouldn't allow it. My clothes were mostly black. I liked pink hair but I wasn't keen on my pink bedroom with fluffy stuffed toys.

My father spent most of his time in the garden, as was his wont. My boxer dog was also banished to the garden. The Yorkshire Terriers didn't like him in the house, apparently.

My stepmother had seven children. With the six of us, that made thirteen, an unlucky number. None of the *children* were at home, except me. They were all grown up, married and had their own families. She once gave me Brains meatballs and I thought that they were really brains. I only found out recently that they were not. I was sick. We never got along. She had wanted another daughter but she didn't want one like me. I didn't fit in well.

I was so glad that she was a nurse. She saved my father's life and gave him (and all of us) fifteen more good years when he had his first heart attack.

The Perfect Fig

Whenever I see Nadia, I cringe and pray for the floor to swallow me whole. Nadia has been blessed by the perfection fairy, who, instead of granting her three wishes, has granted her *every* wish. Nadia is tall and slim with long dark hair which she always wears loose. She never gets hot and flustered and has to tie it up like me. I suppose that is one of the *joys* of early menopause. I am forty-two and she is twenty-six. Oh, to be twenty-six again and do all the things I should have done instead of getting married.

I have never seen Nadia wear the same clothes twice. Clothes that, by the way, never crease. *How is that even possible?* I usually have gravy or custard, or some similar stain down my top and sport leggings with muddy knees. I don't often have time to iron. When I'm not looking after the

116

children, the dog, the cats, the hamster and the house and garden, I am studying.

Nadia drives a black Mercedes. (Don't ask me the model, I drive a Honda!) Unlike other black cars, hers never gets dirty. Not even when it rains. The drops just slide off the polish and leave it looking better than ever. I see Nadia every weekend when she comes with my husband to pick up our three boys. She is my ex husband's new wife and she is perfect.

How much hair can one dog lose? It seems like I spend most of my life hoovering, sweeping and mopping. I have just washed the kitchen floor and the boys come running in from the garden with muddy shoes. I groan, as inwardly as I am able, and begin again. I am so tired. It isn't easy having three boys under eight. Joshua is seven and the twins, Freddy and Harry, will be five next Saturday. I am also close to completing my thesis, *Figs, the 'Fruit' of Mythology*. Life is, erm, fun I suppose. If I had to describe our life in one word, yes, I'd probably say *fun* or, if I were being honest, *chaos.*

My ex-husband is a car salesman. Or, rather, he owns the business. We had to scrimp and save and make a lot of sacrifices when we first moved to Italy to build things up from scratch. Both our families thought that we were crazy when we announced that we were taking the boys to Italy to open a car showroom and so that I could study figs! We were just beginning to enjoy the *fruits* of our labour, and along came Nadia with her pert 20-something-year-old breasts and her Latin tattoo. It says, *Audax at Fidelis* (Bold yet Faithful). Faithful my arse!

Nadia walks as though she is on a catwalk. She wears four-inch heels, as she never has to rush, unlike me. Her nails are always freshly manicured. *Butterfly breath with baby sparkles, No.16 by Esterel,* she told me once. I am sure she was being kind but that information is useless to me. By the time I have cleaned the house, made the beds, done the shopping, made us a meal and trimmed the hedge, my nails are always split and broken.

I would kill for a job in an office and somebody else to make my lunch and clean my house. I study in the evenings, or when the boys are away. Usually one, or all, of them has a cold and is unable to go. That's life. I make time. I have almost finished.

My fascination for figs began when I was a little girl. We used to spend the summer in Miglionico in the South of Italy with my maternal grandparents. My grandfather would always tell me stories and pull the succulent green bulbs from the trees for me to taste. He would open them up and show me the red insides. They were sweet and juicy, and delicious. For me, they will always be the taste of summer.

Nonno Gino told me how a special type of wasp pollinates the figs and how they are not really a fruit at all. Over the summer, I would listen eagerly to his stories while my grandmother brought me dried figs, and biscuits and even fig ice cream. I still have her recipe for fig jam written in dialect. I treasure it.

The twins are five today! *Where have those years gone?* I have four packets of balloons to blow up. The cake is ready in the fridge. I have baked bite-sized sausage rolls and mini cheese straws and the pavlova is almost ready. I just need to whisk the cream for the topping after I have made the sandwiches. I have another hour before the party starts. I wonder how long it will take me to blow up forty balloons and tie them up outside. My English parties for the kids are always a huge success. You'd be surprised how many sausage rolls an average Italian can eat!

I have always loved the relationship that Italians have with food and nature. It must have come from all those summers in Miglionico as a girl. I smile to myself as I remember my grandfather telling me how to pronounce the word fig in Italian. FicO he would say and make me repeat it. Then he would laugh and tell me never to pronounce it with an A. Wide-eyed, I would ask him why and he would laugh again and tell me because it was a naughty word. When I was older, I asked my mother and she explained that it was a vulgar word for a woman's genitals. She had not said the word *genitals*. She had just pointed. How we laughed.

I am only on my seventh balloon and starting to perspire rather a lot when I hear the doorbell. It's Nadia. She is alone. I haven't got time to ask her where Robby is before she bursts into tears. I take her through to the kitchen and pour her some apple juice. She accepts it gratefully, blowing her nose loudly on a piece of kitchen roll. Her mascara has run and she looks like a very sad panda.

In between sips of juice and great big sobs, she manages to tell me what is wrong. They have been trying for a baby for ages and she just got the tests back. She doesn't say, but I surmise that she is not able to conceive. I tell her that there are other options. I am sure that her gynaecologist will already have said this, but it seems to calm her a bit. I give her a packet of balloons to blow up and tell her that they could try in vitro like we did with the twins. She looks surprised. I wonder why Robby has never told her.

She is saying that I am the first person she thought of talking to. She is saying that I am such a good friend who has always treated her with kindness. She is saying that all she wants in life is to be a stay-at-home mum like me. She can't wait to have Robby's baby and now it seems that she might not be able to. My heart breaks for her. My boys are my life.

We sit drinking juice and blowing up balloons until the first guests arrive. Nadia ties up her hair and whisks the cream for the pavlova as I chat to them in the garden. It's a cloudy afternoon. Nadia and I have a long road ahead of us but I will get her through this. It would be nice to have a little girl in the family. I'm sure the boys would love a little sister, or another brother.

Nadia comes out to join us in the garden. She has washed her face and combed her hair. She looks perfect. I hug her and whisper that it will all be ok. I'll be there for her. She hugs me back and smiles, at last. I see Robby coming down the hill, his arms full of presents and I wave to him. The boys tear around the garden with their friends. The sun is starting to peep through the clouds.

Nadia stays after the party to help me clear up. That is so kind of her. I am exhausted. Robby has taken the boys to his mother's. More cake and presents! When we have put the last of the dishes in the dishwasher, Nadia asks me about my thesis. I am taken aback. I didn't even know that Robby had told her about it.

I grab a plate of fig biscuits and a couple of mugs of tea and we go out into the garden and sit under the fig tree. She seems fascinated when I tell her about Demeter, the Greek goddess of agriculture and fertility. I reach up to the tree and pick the perfect fig for her. She seems touched. As I smile at her, I notice that she has pavlova on her blouse.

***

As mentioned in the preface, I reached up one day to pick a lovely round fig from the tree on the terrace, only to discover that it was in fact a lightbulb. I thought that it was so funny. I told my friend and she said, *the perfect fig* and I thought that it was the perfect title for another collection of stories. Usually I have stories and no title. In this instance, I had a title and no story. It took me a long time to think of one.

I did a little research on figs in mythology and as a symbol of fertility and came up with this story. It is complete fiction. My ex husband has not remarried. He has a partner who is older than him, not younger. I have never met her and the character in my story is not based on her or anyone else I know. I simply worked back from the fig to the goddess of fertility to this scenario.

Nor did I or do I have an Italian grandfather. Though I have always felt that I belonged in Italy.

House-haunting in Italy

The agent answered a phone call and then rushed off somewhere, leaving us standing on a medieval bridge looking out at a deep valley below where sheep and goats were grazing and feral cats were lying in the sun. 'Urgente!' he called over his shoulder. 'Very importante! I go.' The owner of the house did not appear at all perturbed when we arrived alone for the viewing and told her what had happened. 'Italy.' She shrugged. She told us that she was French but had lived in Italy for many years.

'It's just fine,' she said. 'Let's have some prosecco on the terrace. She held out a delicate hand to greet us. 'I am the owner, Charlotte De La Cour. Welcome to my home, The Mandarine.' She was obviously someone who took things in her stride. Disappearing behind a pale green door to *get some nibbles*, she left us to look leisurely around the entrance to the house. There was a stairway and long corridor covered by old red brick arches. A beautiful wrought iron gate led the way up just a few steps. Each one was embellished with plants or objects of interest collected, presumably, over the years that the lady had lived here.

We sat at the top of the steps on the low stone wall and looked out over the cobbled courtyard below. It was full of interesting doorways and nooks and decorated with brightly coloured chairs and tables, and plants. We looked at each other happily and knew instantly that this was the home we had dreamt of. And to think that we had not yet been inside the house! 'This is it,' my wife said, and I agreed. This was definitely the one we had been looking for.

When Charlotte returned, she led us through another painted door, this time turquoise, onto the most amazing walled terrace with the roof completely removed so that it was open to the sky. 'The Arabic terrace', she said. We sat on mismatched brightly coloured chairs at an orange table and looked around us. The floor was paved with the original tiles in triangles of faded pink and cream. The walls were the palest pink. They contrasted perfectly with the stunning blue of the sky.

There was a water fountain on one wall, a goddess which I failed to recognise, perhaps the Roman goddess of the sea? A beautiful antique fireplace took pride of place on another wall. Huge terracotta plant pots full of olive bushes and palms and a variety of flowers were dotted strategically around the terrace and amongst them, more feral cats stretched happily in the sun. This was not the place we had dreamt of. It was far beyond our wildest dreams.

Charlotte brought glasses and wine, and dishes of glistening olives and homemade crisps and cheese-straws and other delights for our palates. The wine was superb and the company was delightful. Charlotte was charming. She seemed very young to have made such a beautiful place. She could not have been older than twenty-two or twenty-three. She was dressed in a 1950s style red and white gingham dress, her strawberry-blonde hair falling in waves over her bare shoulders.

Charlotte was beautiful and full of energy. She seemed to adore the house and showed us round proudly, rushing from one room to the next, laughing and chatting freely. My wife, Isabella, was smiling. It had been a long time since I had seen her smile. This could be the place. This could be the place to get our lives back on track. I was sure of it. Isabella seemed to be too.

We spent the rest of the afternoon looking around the house and then chatting on one of the balconies. The insides were as beautiful as the outsides. Stone walls and free-standing bathtubs and beautifully tiled floors. It was breathtaking. Obviously, an awful lot of work had gone into building the place up and making it just right.

Before we left, I asked Charlotte why she had decided to sell. I was not worried that there might be some hidden problem with the house. She seemed like too nice a person to do that. I was just astounded that anyone who lived in such a magical place could ever leave it. 'It's a long story', she said and left it at that. I felt uncomfortable about pressing her further.

The following day we met up with our agent in a little square in town. He insisted on buying us lunch to make up for his having had to rush off the previous day. It wasn't necessary, but he would not take *no* for an answer. He ordered for us all. More delicious fayre arrived for us to sample, and more wine. We tucked in enthusiastically to great bowls of pasta.

There were still four properties left to see and our agent was eager to take us. One was slightly north, near Matera (the city built on rocky cliffs with caves dug into the sides making up homes and museums and hotels), the other three were further south. He was not pleased when we told him we didn't want to see them. We had already decided.

Enrico, our agent, continued to enthuse about the other properties while we ate our lunch in silence. Our minds were made up. There was no point. For some reason, he was trying to put us off buying the beautiful Mandarine house that had stolen our hearts. As we drank our coffee and thanked him for lunch, we said we would like to put in an offer, without delay. That was when he told us the story of the house.

The owner was selling it because it was haunted. We laughed. 'Haunted?' 'Yes. She can have no peace in this house.' He pronounced the word *peace* to sound like peas and we both tried not to laugh, imagining Charlotte trying desperately to eat peas in her house but finding that they always disappeared before she could put them on her fork. The things he was telling us sounded ridiculous and didn't put us off in the least.

The following Sunday, we went back to the house to talk to Charlotte again, to take some measurements and to tell her that we had decided to put in an offer. As we walked up to the iron gates, a stranger with grey hair tied in a low chignon came towards us. She walked down the stone steps slowly and with great difficulty, holding on to the wall with one hand and using a stick to steady herself with the other. This elderly lady held out her hand and said, 'Pleased to make your acquaintance. I am Charlotte De la Cour, the owner.'

***

This is a description of The Mandarine, one of the houses belonging to my friend, Martine. She rents it out over the summer and has no intention whatsoever of selling it. She loves the house and I do too. It is amazing. If you are looking for somewhere to stay in Basilicata and want a real taste of Southern Italy and delicious cuisine, this is the place for you!

I realise that she is featuring in a lot of my stories, but during the last six months, she is just about the only person I see. Luckily, she is amazing and I never tire of her company. We met through a Facebook group for British people living in Italy and the more I found out about her home and her life, the more I thought that she was really living my dream life.

I came to Basilicata on holiday before Covid struck and spent time with her. We got on well. I think it is impossible not to get on with her. I moved south in April 2022 to live in another of her little houses, The Bergamot, in order to use it as a writing retreat, and the rest is history as they say.

Ps. I don't think the house is haunted. She has never mentioned it.

.

Scratch

She had spent the first part of her life waiting and hoping for an opportunity to come along. The second part had been spent regretting the first part. She felt that her life had been empty and worthless and had not been worth living. One day, she caught her reflection in the bathroom mirror and recognized her mother. She had been expecting it to happen but she thought it would have been more gradual. It had been a shock. It had not been enough of a shock to shake her from complacency. She died thinking that her life had been pointless.

Menopause had signalled the end to any hopes of children but had not stopped the cyclical nature of her life. She thought perhaps she was influenced by the moon and the tides. She liked sunsets not sunrises. She waited for the moon. She spent her nights awake and began to sleep during the day. She took tranquillizers to shut out the noise of her neighbours. They were a mean bunch.

When she inherited her mother's money and a villa in the South of France, she had thought she might now be more of a catch. But she had caught nothing. There were, apparently, *plenty of fish in the sea*. Her sight was waning and she could not see them. Her *bait* did not work.

She thought of travelling to France to see the villa again. She had spent summers and the occasional weekend there as a child but she did not remember it. Her passport had expired and, somehow, she never got round to renewing it. The photographs her mother's solicitor had sent her were enough to keep her regrets alive.

Death had been cruel and slow. She had expected to go quickly as had been the case with those family members she had known. Her mother had died in the garden. Her father had died in a car accident. Her only aunt had died in childbirth. She had always thought of dying whilst giving birth as something that happened in books or films or in the distant past. It had never occurred to her that childbirth could be fatal even in modern times.

Instead, she started to feel ill and took to her bed. She was to remain there for years. She had helpers who came to wash and feed her and talk to her as though she were a child. They smiled and nodded politely when she said she had a villa in France. She thought of writing a will. She could not think of a single person worthy of receiving her worldly-goods. She thought that she would die without ever having made the slightest difference to anyone's life. But she was wrong.

One November morning, Maureen arrived to wash and feed her next client. She rang the bell, waited a discreet amount of time before entering, as she had been told to do. She had never been entirely sure about how long a *discreet amount* was. When she had first started doing the job, it had been a decidedly longer amount of time than it was now. Perhaps a few seconds. Long enough to find the right key and glance around the scruffy garden with disdain.

Maureen had never found one of her clients dead before but she knew the procedure to follow. She took it in her stride. As long as she was paid for her time, she did not much care. It always surprised her that people thought of her as being kind because she was in a caring profession. She was more cold than kind. She had switched off in order to cope with the misery and odour of expiring life.

Despite her cold demeanour, Maureen was not an entirely bad person. She had lived her life decently and, for the most part, honestly. It had been her rule, but there had been just one exception. She didn't like this client. She was a cantankerous old crow. The old bird said that she had inherited a villa in the South of France from her mother. She would often take out a faded black and white photograph and show it to Maureen.

Maureen's second husband had just died from a heart attack and she had a disabled daughter to care for. A villa in the South of France might solve all her problems. She tried to get in the old bat's good books by smiling and listening to her stories. She brought her the occasional custard cream and sometimes a drop of rum.

It was all to no avail. The woman was as cold as the stones in the graveyard and, as that was where she was heading, Maureen thought she might help her along by mixing up her medication just a little. But first, she must find a way to get the woman to write a will. It was not easy.

Then, before her task could be accomplished, the woman had died on her. As inconsiderate in death as she had been in life.

Maureen had looked quickly around the shabby terraced abode and found some samples of the old woman's handwriting in the form of several shopping lists written on card from old cornflakes packets. There was nothing for it. Instead of persuading the silly cow to write a will, she would now have to forge one. Maureen was most displeased.

The end result was good, though she did say so herself. The wobbly hand and uncertainty of the words would be attributed to the difficulty of her client's dying moments. Maureen left the pen on the floor and put the paper under the woman's hand where it was sure to be discovered.

The doctor who had been called out, had removed the letter, put it in his jacket pocket without so much as a glance and forgotten about it. He had been up much of the night with his ailing mother. He was tired. When his wife had sent the jacket to be dry-cleaned before being put away for the season some months later, the lady in the shop had removed the letter and left it on the counter.

On Friday evening, in a bit of a hurry, Mrs Dalbrady called in to pick up her daughter's freshly cleaned wedding dress. The 'will' had mistakenly got folded up in the flimsy plastic covering of the flouncy white meringue-like dress and been carried along Church Street for a good distance before detaching itself and falling onto the pavement. Its whereabouts from that moment are a mystery.

Maureen waited in vain for her inheritance. There was nothing she could do. She hated her job. Her dreams of sun and Sauvignon in the South of France had been quashed. She had told her employers about the note in the client's hand, but no trace of it had ever been found. The doctor, having realised his mistake, had kept quiet and denied all knowledge.

Maureen was furious. She trudged from her car to the local shop and bought herself a scratch card with her last £5. It was a lot of money but the prize was worth it. She imagined using her winnings to buy a villa in the South of France and the monthly income that accompanied it, to finance the lifestyle to which she couldn't wait to become accustomed.

She did not win the big prize, but £50. *Better than a smack in the face with a wet fish* she thought to herself and headed back to the shop to buy ten more tickets. It was raining heavily and she didn't see the car that hit her until she was almost under it.

A passerby, who had seen the card fall from Maureen's hand, picked it up. It was a winning ticket but not enough money to make a difference to his life. He decided that, instead of cashing it in, he would exchange it for five tickets at £10 each.

Doctor Jeremy Smythe-Crawshore was flabbergasted to win the top prize - £500,000 and a jolly handsome monthly income. It could be topped up nicely with the money he would receive from taking early retirement. He was starting to become forgetful and, after years of dedication to his profession, he thought it would be nice to live out the rest of his life with his wife and his cat in a lovely villa that he had seen for sale in the South of France.

***

When my adoptive mother died, I did not inherit a single thing, nor did I question why, until many years later. I do not know what became of her jewellery or other possessions. She was never spoken of again. Although I did not care much for her, I found it sad that she was just removed from our lives. She had a beautiful amethyst bracelet that I would have loved to keep. Sadly, she did not possess a villa in the South of France.

I once lived in a villa in the country in Italy. It was enormous and a lot of hard work. So, be careful what you wish for! I did the cooking, the cleaning, the washing and ironing. I cut the grass and trimmed the hedges. There were an awful lot of hedges. I even cleaned and tidied the weeds and brambles on the private road leading up to it. My neighbours would drive past and tell me I was doing a good job! We had a confining strip of land in common with our neighbour down the hill. He was forever suggesting that I plant fruit trees on it.

There was never any time for sun or Sauvignon.

Love Thy Neighbour

'You should plant fruit trees,' he said as he leaned over our railings. My neighbour was back again. He seemed to have an obsession with fruit trees. I wasn't frightened. Even if I was on my own during the day, I had the dogs. He looked harmless enough but I never invited him in.

He came to tell me to plant fruit trees so many times that eventually I grew tired and lied to him. I told him that I didn't eat fruit. He looked devastated. The following day he came and rang the bell. He told me that the tall trees in the garden of the house across the road were dangerous. He said that they would fall on our house and kill us.

My husband said that he was probably drunk or crazy and to ignore him. We laughed about it but when I was swinging in the hammock looking up at the sky, I couldn't help but study the trees across the road and wonder if he was right.

Autumn came and winter. I didn't see my neighbour and I forgot about the trees. In the spring, my husband was diagnosed with cancer. His illness was mercifully quick. His skin was suddenly baggy and his eyes circled with dark red. He lay on the sofa in an old grey jumper. It smelled disgusting but he refused to change. He smoked one cigarette after another, holding them between his orange fingers. His breath smelt foul. Putrid. As though something were rotting inside of him. It was.

'I always knew I would go first,' he said one day. He said he was glad that he would never have to live without me. When he got too sick to walk, our neighbour came and helped me. He didn't ask, just came round. He did my shopping and cut my grass, and helped me wash my husband. He helped me with the feeding tubes. He told me he had been a nurse before he retired.

My husband died in June. My neighbour came and leant on the railings. 'You should plant a fruit tree,' he said. I did. I planted an apple tree for my love.

***

Dedicated to the neighbour who wanted me to plant fruit trees. Fortunately, the rest of the story is complete fiction.

When he told me that the trees in the garden of the house on the road above us would fall onto our roof and kill us, I was terrified. After I had spent months doing up the house in order to sell it and was looking forward to swinging in the hammock and drinking the odd pina colada, I found that I could no longer enjoy it for worrying.

I hope that the new owners are enjoying all my hard work and that the trees never fall on them. I miss my home and Harley, my crazy Labrador, misses the garden. He loved running around and we had such lovely neighbours. When I moved back in, one of them brought me zucchini fritters. Another brought me fresh eggs from his hens. The neighbour on the other side of the road broke into my house by removing the shutters the day I locked myself out!

I have always had extremes as far as neighbours are concerned. They have either been wonderful or terrible.

Wherefore Art Thou?

She found herself still alone at the ripe old age of twenty-six and, despite her friends and family telling her that she was only young and there was time, she was adamant that she really must find herself a man.

Her dance class partner, Lynnette, had shown her how to use an online dating site and helped her upload her picture and write a brief description. Now she was waiting patiently for replies. Well, not too patiently, if truth be known. Her stomach was just a little tight but perhaps that was the cheddar and caramelized onion bap and the mini cheesecake that she'd devoured on her lunch break.

She kept checking her phone on the train journey home. Still nothing. She had filled in all the information and chosen the best photo she could find. She wasn't the type to take selfies often. She had filled in her likes, her dislikes, her name and age. She had told them the kind of man she was looking for: tall, dark and intelligent. She thought of him as James, and imagined him in jeans and a navy-blue sweater. She couldn't wait to meet him.

As the train trundled bumpily along, she imagined her future with James. She would finally have somebody to curl up with on the sofa. To eat popcorn with and watch films on Netflix. The thing she missed most was having somebody to hug. She imagined them staying at home a lot but when they did go out, it would be to do simple things, like going for pizza or walking around an antiques fair, or holding hands at the cinema. James would be a gentle giant. He would cry at sad films but pretend it was just his eyes watering. She was convinced that he was out there somewhere. The other half to complete her apple and make her whole at last.

The train drew slowly into the next station. It was not too busy tonight and she had found a seat near the window. She gazed out at the grey towns creeping by and thought about when she would take James home to meet her parents. At long last, she would have a partner to take to Sunday lunches with all the family.

James would be the perfect gentleman. He would compliment her mother on her Yorkshire puddings and accept a second and a third. He would talk about rugby to her father. Her mother would adore him and say she loved his jumper. Her father would invite him to go up to Bath to see a match together.

Then she would meet James's family and they would be besotted with her. His mother would say that she was the daughter she had never had and his father would smile quietly and nod. They would invite her on their annual September holiday to their villa near Cannes. She imagined herself walking around little fishing villages and artistic hideaways with cobbled streets, hand-in-hand with James. In the evenings, they would sit and eat delicious French dishes followed by crepes Suzette outside romantic bistros. She had never been to France but she had studied the language at school and her Aunt Betty had once made her crepes.

By the time the train was slowing down to pull into her station, Hawley Green, she had already planned the wedding and chosen names for their three children, two girls and a boy or, Clare, Lydia and Thomas as she now thought of them.

Her phone pinged and she hurried down the steps and sat on a bench. She held her handbag between her knees to look at her phone. She was worried about somebody stealing it. At last! There was a message from a certain GoodLove914. She opened it eagerly. It read: *Face is nice. What's your body like?*

Stefan's workmate had talked him into joining a dating site. He said he was sick of seeing him moping around after Hannah left him. They had been together for four years and when she'd left he had been in shock. It was only normal that he needed time to get over it, but perhaps seven months was long enough.

He had loved Hannah and thought that they were happy. When she had moved in with him, he had been ecstatic. He was saving up to buy her an expensive engagement ring and ask her to marry him. Even though he was only 28, he loved the idea of having his own little family. He couldn't wait to be a Dad. He imagined taking the kids to the park to play football and teaching them to ride their bikes. He would be a good Dad, not like his own.

Things weren't going too badly during the week. He had his job to keep him busy and his friends. A couple of nights a week, a group of them would go to the Green Man and have a curry and a couple of beers. On Sundays his brother often invited him round for a roast dinner with all the trimmings. His sister-in-law was not a great cook but it was nice of them to think of him. But, seeing them cooking together all lovey-dovey made him feel sad. He wanted someone special to cook with.

Stefan had been waiting for the right moment to propose to Hannah. He was going to go and ask her father's permission first. That was the way he had been brought up. He knew that it was old-fashioned and sexist but he also knew that Hannah's Dad would have been pleased. He had already booked the flights and a hotel in Verona. He was going to get down on one knee under Juliet's Balcony and pop the question. He wanted to be her Romeo forever.

Despite being 6ft 4in, Stefan was a romantic soul. He had played rugby at university but he was a softy at heart. He loved evenings at home with Hannah cuddling up in front of a soppy film with a bowl of crisps and another of M&Ms. He always pretended he had something in his eye when sad films made him cry. He often imagined what it would be like when Hannah told him that she was expecting and he saw her little bump begin to grow. He wanted two girls and a boy. He hoped the little girl would have Hannah's dimples.

He tried hard to banish all thoughts of Hannah from his mind and imagine life with somebody new. He missed having someone to snuggle up to on cold nights. He thought about what it would feel like having meals out again and just going for a walk with somebody to talk to. He thought about going on holiday with them. This year he could have gone to Barcelona with friends but he had stayed at home. It would only have made him sad being there without Hannah. Nothing was any fun now he was alone. His friends were starting to lose their patience.

The traffic had been lighter than usual and he got home early. As he turned the key in the lock, a feeling of emptiness hit him hard in the stomach. He felt so terribly lonely going back to an empty house. He thought about the cute girl on his dating site. She looked really nice. Somebody who wouldn't hurt him and let him down. She had seemed smiley and warm from her photo and they had similar interests. He looked again. She didn't live far away. She was there in the town next to his. Just a ten-minute drive. He made up his mind to get in touch. He would make the first move.

When Hannah had left, she had said that it wasn't him, it was her. But, she'd also told him that he was boring and too nice and reliable. He was confused. Didn't women want a man who was nice and reliable? He decided to send Snugglepops26 a message. He didn't want to come across as too nice and reliable, so, on the spur of the moment he sent the message: *Face is nice. What's your body like?* He regretted it instantly but it was too late. He hoped that she would answer back so that he could explain himself.

Jessica got her umbrella out of her bag. The sun had gone in and the sky had turned grey. It looked like rain. Before she put her phone away, she deleted GoodLove914.

***

I met the love of my life on a dating app. It all happened quite by accident. I think it was fate, though I don't believe in fate. A friend of mine sent me an SMS one day to tell me that he had written a book and that I should look it up on Google. I didn't know what Google was and I was out at the time. When I returned home, I asked my son and he showed me.

A few days later, I remembered about the book and went to look it up. As I typed the title, *The girl from...* into the search engine, I found lots of sites offering the possibility of meeting girls. I had been separated from my husband for several years and wondered if there were sites for meeting *boys*. It was a long time ago now.

The site I found was very serious. It asked me so many questions that I had to fill it in in a hurry as I ran out of time. I had to go and pick up my son from summer school. When I turned on the computer a few days later, I had hundreds of messages. I was so naïve that I thought I had to reply to them all!

I didn't really think much of any of the men who met my *requirements*. (I had put in age, height and character traits.) The site must have run out of candidates as it began sending me *matches* which definitely didn't meet what I was looking for. Amongst them, I found Riccardo. I loved him.

Horatio

She wanted a baby so badly that, after work, she would go into the toilets and do a pregnancy test even though she hadn't had sex since the last one she'd done. She was obsessed. Once the yearning began, it wouldn't go away. Her every thought was about babies. She saw them everywhere, in their prams, in their mother's arms, with their doting fathers.

She would sit on the bus on her way home from work holding her shirt beneath her jacket as though it were a bump. She started to walk as though she had backache from the weight of the baby. She sat in the park and watched children play. She thought about buying padding or a fake baby bump off the internet.

Alone in bed at night, she would let her feelings wash over her. It felt as though she was being possessed. Something crazy had got inside her brain and was turning her into somebody that she didn't even recognize. She had begun laughing to herself in a sinister way. Well, it was more of a cackle. It was a noise that came from within her but that she couldn't control. It started to get frightening, but at the same time it felt good. It felt good to abandon herself to this evil thing within.

A friend told her how, in order to get pregnant, she had checked her ovulation with a *magic* white stick that she had bought at the chemist. She rushed immediately to buy one. She checked her state of ovulation every day but still didn't get pregnant. That may have been because she hadn't had sex since 1994. In her heart of hearts, she knew that she would have to have sex to have a baby but she still was not ready.

The thought of being with a man again repulsed her. She did not want to feel their drunken breath or their sweaty hands on her smooth skin but time was running out. She was almost thirty-nine.

On Saturday night, she took the plunge and got all dolled up in a short black dress and heels and caught a bus into town. She had no idea where to go. She had never been out in the evening. She walked until she found a pub, The Bramley Arms, and went in.

The bar man was young and eager with tattooed arms and rolled up shirt sleeves. She ordered a glass of white wine and went to sit at one of the round tables near the fireplace. Her shoes stuck to the thick carpet as she tottered across the room. She sat there until her drink had finished then went back and ordered another. Nobody came to talk to her. No men were interested. She was feeling light-headed now so she went out onto the street to get some air. Nobody followed her. She felt invisible. This was not going to be easy. She wished she had enough time and money for artificial insemination.

She could hear music coming from a club across the road, a little further up. She thought she might have more luck there. The club was dark and almost empty. Perhaps it was still early. *It will fill up when the pubs close*, she reasoned to herself. She went to the bar and ordered a glass of white wine. She couldn't afford a cocktail.

As she took her drink and tried to spy a table in the dark, she saw him. He too seemed to be alone. He was sitting near the dance floor. She was sure it was him. She wondered whether to go over and say hello, or whether to just walk by and hope he recognised her. In the end, she lost her nerve and went to sit at the table next to his.

She had never given him much consideration but, at least here in the dark, he was not an unpleasant looking man. He was tall and slim and wore round glasses with black frames. She wished she had brought her own pair with her. She wondered how old he might be and decided that he must be between thirty and forty-five. She thought he might still have a good chance of impregnating her, if only she could attract his attention.

She drank the dregs of her wine, gritted her teeth and got up to dance. Her legs were shaking so much that her knees were literally knocking. She didn't know this song and hadn't danced since she was a teenager but she had been studying the three or four people on the dance floor and was sure that she could do it. The wine had started to cloud her judgement.

As she got onto the floor, the music changed into something that she had actually heard on the radio. Probably at the supermarket whilst doing her weekly shop. It was rather more energetic than she was expecting and whilst she gave it her all, it would have been a lie to say that she had rhythm in her soul. She was all arms and legs. And none of them moved in unison, with the music or each other.

Luckily, though, it had had the desired effect. The Pharmacist, who had sold her a pregnancy test every week for the last two years, had recognized her now and was watching her with a mix of interest and alarm. He was a kind man and he felt it his duty to rescue her but he wasn't sure how. He downed the last of his drink, took a deep breath, and got up to ask her to dance. She was a pretty woman, perhaps a little odd. He wondered why she bought so many pregnancy tests. He had no explanation.

They danced to one song. He had no rhythm either. Then he asked her if she would like a cocktail and she accepted gratefully. They moved away from the dance floor and found a quieter corner. The music was still loud and it was not easy to chat. When they leaned in to hear each other better, he could not help but look down the top of her dress. She did not notice. She was looking at his crotch.

Back at his one-bedroomed apartment above the Chemist's shop, they were struck down by a passion they had not felt for quite some time. It may have been the alcohol, it may have been the music. Dr. Daniel Winterbottom was sure it was caused by pheromones. He was having a chemical reaction to this female of the species. They mated on the couch.

Daniel made coffee. He was not entirely sure what to do now. He was beginning to regret not having used protection. Especially when he had a drawer full of condoms in the bedroom. But it was too late now. His guest was looking embarrassed and he wished he knew what to say. He gave her the nicest mug and let her sleep in his bed. She did not invite him to sleep with her, and for that, he was relieved.

The next morning, bright and early, she said she must be on her way. He made her toast and marmalade and asked to see her again. They agreed upon Thursday. They went to the Odeon to see a film that they had both been wanting to watch. It was not bad. Not brilliant but not a disappointment either. They were, if truth be told, happy enough to sit sharing a bucket of popcorn and the occasional observation.

Their affair was brief but pleasant. It ended when she met his five children. Perhaps it had been too soon. He could see that she was overwhelmed. She had been feeling nervous all day but she knew she must get this over with. Daniel had been married twice and had two sons from his first marriage, and a son and two daughters from his second. She had told him of her desire to have children and he had seemed enthusiastic.

Daniel had been ready to pop the question. He thought it might be a case of third time lucky.

But first, he wanted her to meet his children. They were the most important thing in his life and he needed to be sure that they would get on. The day had gone well, or so he had thought. They had gone to the park and had a picnic on the grass. Then they had fed the ducks and the swans. She had seemed to enjoy herself and the children obviously liked her. They jumped all over her and tugged her this way and that. As the day wore on, though, he saw that she was struggling a little with the situation.

The truth was that she was feeling somewhat nauseous. She thought it might be the salmon paste. The children were extremely loud and, after their food, distastefully sticky. The boys were rather rough and the little girls were very clingy. She was not having a pleasant day at all. She could not imagine many things worse than spending her future this way.

She decided to leave Daniel. He had sounded very hurt. No, no. She was quite sure.

There was no point in discussing it further. She would no longer need his assistance at the Pharmacy. Her desire to have a baby had evaporated in the summer heat. She was cured of her obsession.

The following Saturday, she caught the number 47 bus into town and went to the pet shop on Penny Street, near the bank. She was delighted with her purchase. She adored him already. They would be a little family. From now on, no more silly ideas. It would be just the two of them. He was a darling boy and no trouble at all. He would sit quietly and wait for her to come home from work. She decided to call him Horatio. Horatio the hamster.

***

When I was a girl, I always imagined myself growing up, getting married and having a very large family. I probably wanted to reproduce the happiness of my childhood. The idea of having children, though, was always *at some later date*. I worked hard and enjoyed my job. I put my career first and then my husband's career.

Then, quite suddenly, my biological clock began to tick. My friend, who is Brazilian, had the most beautiful baby girl. When I saw her, I instantly wanted a baby. I wanted a boy and was lucky enough to have one. An American friend saw him and wanted a baby too. She was also blessed with a beautiful baby boy. How strange is the ticking of the biological clock.

I have never possessed a hamster.

Glasses

People think it must be lovely to have a twin. Sometimes it is. Sometimes it isn't. I think it's a question of identity. There are friends and even some family members who couldn't tell us apart when we were little so they called us both *Twin* or, collectively, *The Twins*. It's nice to feel a part of something that extends beyond yourself and yet, at times I think it would be better to be just me. To be just Penny.

So, we shared the same name and we shared the same bed. We used to read together and look at the pictures together and dream together. When we read Cinderella, Silvia said that when we grew up and had big breasts, we would lace them into corseted ball gowns. Hers would be pink and mine would be pale yellow. Sadly, we both grew tall and skinny. No big breasts, no ball gowns. No Prince Charmings waiting to whisk us away to a better life.

That was about the time when my Mum started calling us Pen and Sil. Get it? Pencil! Ha flaming ha. It's not funny when you're twelve and looking down on the rest of your class at boarding school.

We weren't completely identical; Silvia liked school. I didn't. They used to weigh and measure us in Biology classes and it was humiliating to be the tallest *and* the lightest. Our school was like going back in time to the Victorian age. They asked us when our menstrual period started and kept a record in a blue notebook. I left school without ever telling them that mine had started the summer before I went there. I always did like my privacy. Silvia was more outgoing.

Silvia was the popular twin and I was the quiet one. When we went into class, the other girls would shout for Silvia to go and sit with them. I was the twin who cried herself to sleep in the dark with the covers over her head. A group of them beat me regularly with rolled up magazines. They would stick out their feet and try to trip me. They put dirty knickers in my gym bag. They spat in my dinner. School was my living hell.

One Christmas, as my mother was hanging striped metal sugar canes on the tree, I told her what had been happening. She listened carefully then went very quiet. After a while she simply said, 'You must have misunderstood'. And that was that. I never mentioned it again. When we got back to school, somebody had peed on my cookery apron and stolen my tennis racket. I got a note for being without it and a letter to my parents. My mother was furious. Our rackets had been gifts from a friend of hers who had played professionally in her youth and they were both autographed.

Silvia might have been Mum's favourite but I was Dad's. He called me Lucky (his lucky penny). I didn't feel very lucky back then. I don't feel lucky even now. I *did* win a raffle at school once. Each child had to put in a gift and then people bought tickets at the school open day to raise money for the roof repairs. I won a pretty, pink hairbrush, comb and mirror set. When they realized that my parents had donated it, I had to give it back and pick another ticket. Number 47 won me a box of crackers for cheese that had been opened then re-sealed with sticky tape! They were soft. Silvia won a voucher – ice skating and then pizza for two. Of course, she didn't take *me*. I was both upset and relieved. I find it difficult to keep my footing when walking. I do not find ice appealing.

Years later when I was married to Teddy, I had the winning ticket on a ferry from Calais to Dover. We were on a weekend break to celebrate our first wedding anniversary and were so excited.

My husband thought it might be a car or a cruise. We won a £5 voucher for the Duty Free. The cheapest item was £5.99 and they were closing when we got there. We chose two whisky glasses and had to pay an extra 99p for the pleasure. I don't drink whisky but, somehow, I acquired them during the divorce. I use them for sangria in the summer.

We have *moved on* as Teddy says. What he means is, *he* has moved on to his twenty-four-year-old secretary, Janice. Twenty-four, coincidentally, is the number of years that I dedicated to our farce of a marriage. But I'm not bitter. I have two lovely whisky glasses to remember him by and I am a huge fan of sangria. Olé!

***

I am not a twin, but I have friends who are. Though they are *identical*, I find them extremely

175

different, and have never got them mixed up. I know other people who have and they were indeed referred to as *The Twins*. I wondered how they felt about this, though we never spoke about it. They have very different characters and I adore them both. I have always thought it would be great to have a twin.

I never went to boarding school. I was never picked on at school, though I did win a voucher on a ferry once.

Dirty Linen

Elise had a terrible habit of washing her dirty linen in public. Everyone present at the coffee morning at 47 Breston Way knew the ins and outs of her life in minute detail. They were all becoming rather bored with it. They had listened to her moan about her 'difficult' daughter and her 'snooty' mother-in-law, her 'useless' gardener and not to mention, the 'terrible' teachers at the school their children all frequented. But, her favourite topic of conversation was Craig, her 'cheating' husband.

This morning Elise was peculiarly quiet and looking rather dowdy in her beige shift-dress and pearls. Not at all her usual self. Amanda offered her a piece of coffee and walnut cake, hoping to cheer her up. The tray bake had been cut into bite-sized squares, all iced, and topped with a single walnut. She used Camp liquid coffee as her mother and grandmother had done before her and, probably, her great grandmother too.

Amanda felt a little bit sorry for Elise. The other mothers were quite unkind behind her back and she was not an unpleasant person for all her faults. She had brought Amanda a lovely bunch of flowers picked from her own garden and tied carefully with a cream-coloured ribbon. Elise didn't like to go anywhere empty handed.

Amanda topped up her coffee. She was trying out a new blend from the little coffee shop, in the alley next to Oxfam. She seemed to remember that it was from Ethiopia. She had once sponsored a child from there through the nuns at Our Lady's. A little girl called Tighist. She received letters and photos, and updates on her progress at school. At Christmas, she would post clothes and other goodies to try to brighten up her little life. The girl had disappeared when fighting had broken out again between Ethiopia and Eritrea. She often wondered what had become of her. The nuns had offered her another child which had seemed callous but which was probably just being practical. She had declined.

The conversation had, as so often happened, got around to holidays. It would soon be half-term. Anya and Ben were taking the twins to see their grandparents in Wales as usual. Ella was going to be on her own as it was the boys' turn to stay with their dad. She was flying over to Portugal to see her sister and her new niece. Lynda and Jamal were staying at home. They were having work done on the conservatory roof.

When Amanda arrived from the kitchen with another pot of coffee, they were discussing men and, in particular, husbands. Elise perked up a little after her coffee and started telling them about the *beastly* things that Craig had done since their last coffee morning.

He was always leaving toothpaste stains in the bathroom sink. One day he had forgotten to put the kitchen scissors away in the drawer. On Thursday, he had eaten out at lunchtime with clients and had forgotten to tell her. She had thrown his cottage pie, wilted greens in Dijon mustard dressing and red cabbage into the kitchen bin, plate and all.

The group of mothers listened to these complaints. They were used to it. They even found themselves agreeing with Elise. Not because they thought that poor Craig's behaviour was unacceptable, but because they wanted Elise to stop. They felt awfully uncomfortable talking about him behind his back this way. They were all rather fond of Craig and disliked Elise with varying degrees of intensity.

They were horrified when Elise began telling them about her sex-life. Each one of them was inwardly begging her to stop. She complained about his premature-ejaculation, and how he always told her not to move. She said she was quite grateful that they didn't have sex often as she had studied every inch of their bedroom ceiling and could take no more.

The mothers were shuffling uncomfortable in their seats. The situation really was excruciating. As Elise told them what a sloppy kisser Craig was, they sipped their coffee and looked down, suddenly finding their own shoes incredibly interesting.

When Elise announced that she had had enough and had decided to leave Craig, they all seemed rather pleased. 'He is terrible in bed,' she wailed. 'Oh, I wouldn't say that!' the others exclaimed in unison.

***

I have never been to a coffee morning in my life. I can think of few things I would enjoy less. I am not a fan of gossip and have no gossipy friends, at least none that come to mind. The idea for this story was a joke my sister-in-law told me. I thought it was quite funny.

As far as I know, my ex husband never cheated on me. He is the faithful type.

The Winter Child

When you were little you once asked me, 'Why did you make me born in February?' and I laughed at first. I laughed at the innocence of your question and your funny English. Then I started to feel guilty. I wonder if all mothers feel guilty or whether you have just been particularly good at manipulating me. Even then. Even when you were so small,

I felt guilty for having denied you all those summer birthday parties. We had the villa and the garden and the money. But you were born in February. So you had your birthdays at the village pizzeria like all the children who were not born in summer or who did not have a garden for all the children to run around in or a pool to swim in.

You were only ever happy outside. You liked to swim and climb and kick a football around the garden on your own. You once asked me, 'Why do you not make me a brother?' Somehow, you thought that a brother would arrive fully-grown and ready to play football and swim with you. Later, you would say that you were happy to be an only child. You didn't want to share me with anyone.

I felt guilty for not giving you a big family and a happy childhood. I wanted to recreate what I had had. But that was impossible. My family is far away or dead and we are alone here. Just the two of us. We are foreigners in a land that doesn't want us. I hope you know that my family would have loved you if they'd been here. If we'd been there.

There were only a few of us who made it. Mostly men. Young men. Good sons going to work in a land they thought would be their salvation. Dreams in their heads of abundance and happiness. Hope in their hearts. So many died. They took care of me. They gave me water first and what little food there was. They saw my belly swollen with you and they tried to protect us.

I did well for us my son. I have a big house and a nice car. We have nice clothes. I paid for your education. I *got lucky* and married a good man. I *hung up my hat* so they say here. An old man. I know how people looked at us and thought I wanted his money. But he was a good man. A lawyer. He fought for our rights. He died fighting. All dead men are good. We shall say no more for ours is not to comment.

I always wonder why you left. It's somewhere I've never been and know little about. You don't tell me much. So far away. I think you did the right thing. You were never going to be accepted here. I will never be accepted here. I stay because I am too tired to go. I stay because I don't know where to go. I stay because I have become unacceptable amongst my own people and have always been unacceptable amongst these people.

I pray every day. I am thankful for you. For the time we had. For the joy you gave me. For the way you lit up my world. Those are my memories. More precious than any possession. More precious than a machine to wash my pots and pans. More precious to me than silk dresses and my platinum rings.

Now all I have is time. Often too much of it. Sometimes too little. I think of you there and wonder about your life. I imagine my mother back in the home country thinking about me here. Wondering how my life is. I tried to find her. To bring her here, but the rains had come and they were all gone.

***

I hadn't been in Italy very long, perhaps a year, when I met my first boyfriend. His family had a house at the beach on the Riviera. We would go every weekend in the summer. I loved it there. I love large families. He was one of ten children. The house was always full of people and laughter. We would walk to the beach in our flip-flops, ducking to walk under a very low passageway that came up directly on the sand.

One day on the beach, the family introduced me to a friend of theirs. I cannot remember his name now, all these years later, but I remember his smile. We saw him often. He had come across from Morocco on an illegal boat. He had no documents. He sold odds and ends on the beach to make money to send to his family. He slept under one of the bridges nearby. He was always smiling.

I have never had to face such great hardship. My life in Italy is in no way comparable to that of an illegal immigrant. I do, though, know what it is like to be a fish out of water. I have lived in Italy for years but I shall never be Italian. I shall always be a foreigner. I am accepted in my own country, the UK, but I do not recognise it anymore. I remember the way it was when I left.

Would you Like a Willy?

We set off just after lunch (pecorino cheese and pickle on a pumpkin seed bap) to avoid the traffic. Tom said it would take a good three hours to get to the house – there is nothing good about three hours in a car with my husband, I can tell you.

The invitation had arrived in the post. A gold card with purple balloons. My sister, Samantha (Sam), was having a bit of a bash for her fiftieth. My heart sank. I really couldn't think of anything worse. But needs must, duty calls and all that.

Tom drove around all the petrol stations looking for the cheapest fuel. I do understand the need for economy, but surely any saving would have been cancelled out by the extra mileage, wouldn't it? Then, as soon as we got on the motorway, he needed a pee. 'Why didn't you go before we set off?' 'I'm not a child Ruth.' I was tempted to comment, *then why do you insist on acting like one?* But I resisted the urge. I wish Tom had been able to resist his urge. I waited in the car while he queued for the Men's.

We hadn't been back on the road long before he decided he was feeling sleepy and suggested stopping for a coffee at the next services. Give me strength. If only I had a heavy-bottomed frying pan to hand. Though I must admit the apple tart I had with my cappuccino was delicious. 'Would you like to go to the toilet again?' I asked sarcastically. Tom just grunted and strode off back to the car.

Three hours and sixteen minutes of Abba's greatest hits later (knowing me, knowing you, this is going to be a very long weekend), we pulled up outside The Hawthorns. Don't get me wrong. I have absolutely nothing against people who name their houses, but there isn't a tree in sight! Samantha's garden is all crazy paving and low borders.

Sam was standing in the doorway with a huge smile on her face. She'd lost a bit of weight since Christmas but she was still her usual cuddly self. We stayed for a while, left her present (a voucher for a spa weekend for two at The Orchard Lodge), exchanged a few words with my brother-in-law and my niece, Olivia, and set off tiredly for our B&B. Tom had found it somewhere online. My expectations were not high.

The B&B didn't look too bad from the outside and there was off-road parking. The room was fairly pleasant too if you go in for we're-stuck-in-the-nineties floral borders and stenciled furniture.

Tom decided to go out and stretch his legs after the long drive so I put some water in the white plastic kettle and made a mug of tea. Then I lay on the, surprisingly comfortable, bed and read, *How to do your entire skincare regime for less than £45*, in the April edition of a magazine. My entire skincare routine consisted of soap and water.

I had just finished an article about a couple who had fallen in love on a skiing trip to Austria after she had twisted her ankle and he had carried her back to her cabin and called the hotel doctor, when Tom arrived with cream cakes. An iced bun and a jam doughnut. I chastised him for filling us up with sugary stodge before the party instead of thanking him for the lovely gesture. Then I tucked into my creamy jam-filled doughnut.

We arrived back at The Hawthorns fashionably late and found the party well underway. Olivia came and took our coats, sighing and raising her eyes to the ceiling as she did so. She was at the age where she found her mother incredibly embarrassing. Then again, I found Samantha incredibly embarrassing too. My brother-in-law,

Grant, greeted us with a hug and a plate of Ritz crackers with something cheesy on top.

When I eventually found my sister, she was already three sheets to the wind, tongs in one hand, a bowl of ice in the other. 'Would you like a willy?' she repeated as she tonged penis-shaped ice-cubes into everyone's drinks. Cringe. I kissed her on the cheek, wished her happy birthday again and reluctantly accepted a willy in my white wine.

An hour of dancing and party games and three-quarters of a bottle of wine later, the Fireman strippergram arrived. I backed hastily into the corner behind Tom while Sam grabbed hold of the poor stripper by his hosepipe and helped him to undress. Then she sat on his knee and, well, I stopped looking when her hands began sliding up his thighs.

Suddenly the lights went off and Grant came in with the cake. The one giant candle lit up

Sam's happy face and the smiley faces of her friends. With the light back on, it was hideous. Fuchsia pink with turquoise roses and a pile of turquoise macarons on top next to a giant gold number 50.

The cake made me think of my fortieth birthday. I'd been out with Tom to a cheese and wine tasting. When we got back home, a giant bunch of flowers had been left with our neighbour, Anne, across the road. I was so over-come thinking that they were from Tom. It had been both a disappointment and a pleasure to read the card and see they were from Sam. Anyway, Tom must have felt guilty because the next day he arrived with a cake. It said *Happy Fortieth and a Day!* on top.

I had burst into tears. It had seemed like such a mean reminder of something that I had forgotten about already. Looking back, I think he was trying hard to do something nice for me. He just wasn't very good at it and I was over-sensitive.

I was bogged down with work, and always tired. Now I am making excuses.

Sam blew out the candle, which instantly relit itself and everyone, except me, found that hilarious. After the handing out and eating of the cake was concluded, I hoped in vain that the party was over. Wrong. The karaoke began. Lord save me please. I was just wondering whether to hide in the upstairs loo when Sam got up to sing *Girls Just Wanna Have Fun*.

As I stood watching my sister belting out the wrong words in her tone-deaf and very loud voice, a warm feeling suddenly spread through me. I saw how happy my sister was and realised that she is a truly beautiful person. I love her. I looked across at my husband Tom who was still eating his cake and chatting to a woman in a sparkly red dress. She is hanging on his every word, and I thought what a good man he is. I love my husband.

I am truly blessed. I poured myself another glass of wine and popped two willies in it for good measure.

***

When I was seventeen my father told me that the woman I had always thought of as my sister was in fact my mother. It was not really a surprise. I had suspected as much for some time. I went to live with her and her family. It didn't work out well.

Years later, when my own son was five and I was just getting to know my birth mother better, through very long phone calls (she was in Turkey and I was in Italy), she passed away suddenly at Christmastime. It broke my heart. She loved Christmas and she loved parties.

Gifted

Even though she didn't think of herself as being particularly materialistic, she did enjoy presents. She was such a fragile woman, even now, as she was approaching her fifties, and should have been gaining in confidence (according to the magazines she read). A present, to her, was always a sign that somebody had thought of her and considered her worthy of receiving it.

A present meant that somebody had cared enough about her to think about what she would like and had taken the time to go out to the shops and look around until they found exactly what they were looking for. Until they found the thing that would be perfect for her. Or, at very least, they had clicked on Amazon.

She always looked forward to her birthday and to Christmas to receive these affirmations of her worthiness. She always expected great things and was always disappointed. Over the years she had received some truly hideous presents.

Janet sat on her old green sofa with a mug of Horlicks and began to think about presents past. She was only forty-seven but she was starting to have memory problems. She had been to her doctor. The woman had not even listened to her but had taken out her prescription pad and suggested anti-depressants. Janet did not feel depressed.

Janet did not feel happy either. The truth was, that Janet did not feel very much of anything except, perhaps, numb. She was, however, quite sure that she was entirely comfortable with her numbness and had no wish to feel great emotions. She was tired of drama. She had no place in her life for sadness or happiness or desperation. Lordy no.

Life was fine as it was. Janet was a bit of a plodder. She was a widow and had given up her job as a florist to take care of her husband in his last months on God's not very good earth. It had drained her, physically and mentally. She was not entirely sure when she had switched off, but she had. She had no intention of switching back on again.

Janet was doing fine. She just wished she had a better memory. It was getting rather embarrassing. Only the week before she had gone out for a Chinese meal. She had been alone. She was alone. The restaurant had offered a set meal for £15 with a starter, main, side and dessert plus coffee. The drink was extra. Janet had munched her way quite happily through two spring rolls, a bowl of fried rice with chicken curry and a fried coconut pudding, washed down by a bottle of beer. Janet did not drink alcohol as a rule but she was beginning to enjoy the occasional beer or glass of wine. It made her loneliness less lonely sometimes and she thought that she was fitting in. Janet did not want to stand out. She was more of your fitting-in kind of person.

The coffee had been delicious. Janet was very particular about how she liked her coffee and had explained to the girl that she would like the milk apart so she could add her own and she didn't want a saucer. Janet wasn't keen on saucers for some reason that she was unable to fathom. Nor was she a fan of milky coffee.

When the girl came back to take her cup away and ask her if everything had been to her liking, she had asked for another cup of coffee, adding that she would like it made in just the same way. The girl had seemed confused. Janet looked at her and, rather surprised, had explained about the size of the cup and that she didn't want a saucer and that she would like the milk apart, and then she had realised that the woman before her was not the same one.

This lady was much older. She was probably the girl's grandmother. Janet had been worried. She wondered if she was getting some kind of dementia. In the mornings, she did the crossword and her faculties still seemed to be working. It was just her memory. She had started putting her phone in strange places, like in the fridge. She had been surprised to find it on top of the Cheddar and even more surprised that it had still worked perfectly.

She had also started buying too many bottles of shampoo because she could not remember if she had run out or not. One Saturday, Janet had driven into town to do her weekly shop and had gone in to Sainsbury's. She did not need much. Just a few bits. She ended up with two bags of shopping which were jolly heavy.

The following morning, Janet had got up rather late and made herself a nice sausage and bacon *butty* with soft white bread and lots of butter.

She always went to church and did her duty on the Lord's day. Janet was a staunch Catholic. She was also a staunch believer in treating herself to a bacon sandwich once a week. More than once and she would have been guilty of gluttony and that would not have done. But, once a week was fine. It gave her something to look forward to. It also stopped her stomach from rumbling in the dark and empty church.

Janet put on her Sunday dress. It was navy blue. She put on her Sunday cardigan and her Sunday shoes. She took her car keys from her handbag and walked out into a dampish grey English morning. The leaves were falling from the trees and she thought about sweeping the path when she came home. She was careful not to slip. When she reached the end of the driveway and was about to get into her car, she realised that it had gone. She stood dumbfounded, the chilly morning seeping through her cardigan.

Janet rushed back up the path, forgetting about the slippery leaves and went inside to telephone the police. It was the first time she had missed a Sunday morning service for years. Not since she had had her appendix out and had been in her hospital bed eating congealed broth and grey mashed potato instead of the body of Christ. But, the following Sunday she had been there bright and early and despite her aching side, had sung her hymns and crossed herself and drunk Christ's blood.

The police had come within the hour and Janet had been surprised. She had given them the description and the registration number. She could not remember it offhand, but she had it written on her online insurance document. They did not stay for tea, which was rather a shame as she had bought some raspberry creams the day before and would have enjoyed the company.

As she was tucking into her third biscuit and brushing crumbs off her cardigan, her phone had rung. Janet didn't know anyone who would phone her on a Sunday morning. Her mother and her sister would have thought she was at church. Her friends, those few she had, would have been busy with their husbands or their children or their knitting. She wondered whether something might have happened to Granny.

It was the police. They had found her car in the car park at Sainsbury's where she had left it when she had distractedly walked home with her shopping the day before. They told her that she had been very lucky. The joy riders who had stolen it had parked it up and locked it and it did not appear to have so much as a scratch. 'Very odd', Janet said when she went to collect it. She felt bad about lying to the police. She would ask for God's forgiveness when she said her prayers and hoped that they would put her red face down to the cold weather.

After lunch, Janet drove into town and went Christmas shopping as she had planned. She trailed around the shopping centre for several hours going from one shop to the next with her list of presents. She had bought blackberry bath bombs and some hand-cream for her sister, June, and a box of lavender drawer fresheners for Granny. She was just going into Boots to get a foot spa for her mother when she thought to herself that she really must remember to take the car home again. It would not do to mislay it twice on one day.

On Christmas morning, Janet packed her presents into a sturdy plastic bag and set off early to drive to Poulton. It was Aunty Betty's turn to do Christmas this year. Janet was looking forward to it. There would be fourteen of them with Uncle Arthur's side of the family. Lots of presents to open. Janet did love presents.

June opened the door wearing one of Aunty Betty's aprons. Janet was a little miffed that she was not the first to arrive. She liked to help out in the kitchen. June kissed her on both cheeks. Janet tutted and told her she had been spending too much time abroad in those countries that went in for kissing.

Uncle Arthur hugged her and poured her a glass of red wine and laughed when Janet said, 'well I really shouldn't but just the one'. She sang along to one of those new fangled Christmas songs that she didn't know the words to but wanted to show willing.

After lunch, they all sat down to open their presents. Janet was looking forward to it. She was hoping that her sister might have bought her the new paperback book that she had been dropping hints about for weeks. She had no idea what Aunty Betty would have bought, perhaps some warm cashmere tights for winter. She had seen some lovely burgundy ones.

Janet's mother always said she never knew what to get her. The present was wrapped in red and silver paper. It looked very large. Janet hoped it was a hamper with some nice cakes and biscuits, some luxury chocolates and perhaps some unusual pickles and a tin of salmon.

June announced that they had no idea what to get Janet this year so they had all clubbed together and bought one present. She looked very proud of herself. Janet felt a twinge of disappointment. She had been looking forward to opening lots of little presents. Some perfume, some books, perhaps a scarf. She was very easily pleased. In any case, Janet was convinced that it was a hamper and she was quite excited to see what was inside. If they had all bought it together, there would perhaps be real smoked salmon and a bottle of champagne. She was getting ever so excited.

Janet tore the paper away with unbecoming enthusiasm. It was a large box. Not a hamper at all.

Janet read the writing on it. It was an electric blanket. She already had an electric blanket and she had never used it as she was afraid of being electrocuted in her sleep. In any case, she was going into menopause and was often hot. She smiled and thanked them all for the lovely gift.

Christmas was always such a huge disappointment but it would be her birthday in March. She was sure that she would get some lovely presents then.

***

I think that most people know what it's like to receive a present they don't really like or not to receive something that they were really hoping for. As a child, Christmas was so exciting and I received so much that I don't remember being particularly disappointed, except for the time when I got a bike and it was hidden behind the door.

As I got older, I probably asked for what I wanted. I remember asking for a dog and getting a sewing machine. But, it was okay because when I asked for a horse I got a dog and I loved making my own clothes when I was a teenager.

Of course, it can work both ways too. We can disappoint others with our gifts. A friend of mine once bought her mother-in-law a lovely Christmas candle, only for the dreadful woman to offer to give it to her daughter (my friend's sister-in-law, who thought the candle was lovely), because she didn't like it! How very rude.

In order to buy presents that people will like, I often start thinking about Christmas over the summer and getting some ideas. Over the years, I have bought some unlikely gifts. I once wrapped a box of ice-cream-filled chocolates for my father. I had put them in the freezer the night before, but by the time he opened them they had melted. The seven-year-old me was very upset, but now it seems quite funny.

My own mother-in-law once gave me a beautifully soft pale pink sweater. It really was lovely and a perfect fit. I was very touched until she told me that it was something that she'd been given, a recycled gift, and if I didn't like it, she had a whole drawer of things and I could choose something else! Ha ha...

It's also nice to find that the same thought has gone into the present you receive as has gone into the present that you give. I cannot for the life of me remember what I gave my ex husband for our fourteenth wedding anniversary. We were on holiday in Sardinia. I'm sure it was something lovely though. He gave me a lady-shaver! I am one of the world's least hairy people. Also, the damned thing hurt.

In any case, it is the thought that counts, or so they say. Sometimes it is difficult to imagine that very much thought has gone into it. Oh dear, that sounds very ungrateful. Happy Christmas one and all!

Acknowledgements

Thank you to my son, my Sun, Matteo Federico Saveri, for being happy about all of this and trying to help. Thanks for dealing with the technical side of things, again. I am so very sorry, but you know I am a technophobe.

Thank you, yet again, to Martine Greslon-Collins. I wouldn't have written this second book without your enthusiastic encouragement and your constant friendship.

Thanks also to Michele Bowry for telling me about the way you met your husband and giving me permission to turn your story into whatever I wished (*The Cork*). I do hope you like what I have done.

An enormous thank you to all the people who read my last book and gave me feedback, especially those in the *Living in Italy with British*

Roots Facebook group. Your messages have meant so much to me and encouraged me to continue writing. I will not name you all as I would be so sorry to leave somebody out and disappoint you.

Heartfelt thanks to my friends for their support and advice: Genni Gianfranceschi Bertini and Cathy Grigg. Thanks to Rosalind Roberts for your friendship and curiosity. I hope I have managed to answer your questions. Thanks, again, to Anita Summers-Manuzi. We had such a lovely time on the Adriatic coast.

Special thanks to the extremely talented and patient Jill Bissenden for doing the book cover for me. We laughed so much whilst discussing it. To say I love it would be an understatement.

If you have enjoyed these little stories, you may also like:

The Wife in the Wardrobe, S. M. Walker,

a collection of 27 short and very short stories with a twist, including:

- **The Cold Man** – "The day my second husband didn't come home from work, I pretended that he'd decided to stay on the train and go to Venice because that is what he always said he would do one day."

- **The Wife in the Wardrobe** – "I have not caught her out yet but I will. That curve below the curve of her perfect breasts contains the proof of her crime."

- **Innocence** – "That morning he didn't sit on the green bench. He waited in the trees for her to pass. She was alone as usual."

Printed by Amazon Italia Logistica S.r.l.
Torrazza Piemonte (TO), Italy

38913256R00121